OUTPOST 16

written by

A. G. Sinkó

Ezüst Sárkány Publications
Irvington, N.Y.

Special thanks to:

Agnes, Joe, Josef, Wendy, Meg, Suzanne, Karen, Meg, Donna, Milo, and
the rest of my people.

Ezüst Sárkány Publications
125 North Broadway Irvington, N.Y. 10533
Ezust_Sarkany@yahoo.com

ISBN: 978-1-7354293-0-4

OUTPOST 16

1.

Our outpost can only support forty more people. Warren has told the lieutenant and the chief this, and the chief supposedly told his bosses. Yet, the large transport brings fifty children. I don't know where we'll put all these kids. I hope they're not a bunch of cry-babies like the last batch six weeks ago. Warren says some kids are still whining from that group. My job is to check the luggage for any biologicals. No foreign organics except food printer supplies are allowed on the outpost, not even clothes or leather shoes. It's a shame, since some of the stuff the kids wear looks cool, but rules are rules.

There are dark footprints on the gray loading deck. Given their size, they're probably from one of the pilots, but who knows. The new boots aren't supposed to leave marks. More for us to clean.

The white decon area is supposed to hold a hundred people and their stuff, but the room looks packed with kids. Some of them are in regulation suits - yellow for under 16 - some of them are in Old Earth clothes. Anything not destroyed can be recycled.

The computer recording begins: "Please leave your bags outside the door; they will be taken to your quarters shortly.

Please step into the locker room, remove your clothes, and take a shower. Make sure to wash your hair and your feet. When you are finished, new clothes will be provided for you, and you will gather in the debriefing room. Thank you for your cooperation." Most of the ones who just arrived don't have a problem with following these directions. That makes my life easy.

Zip the bio-suit up, turn the vent on, head out the airlock into the decon area. Someone got sweaty in this suit. It smells gross, and the gloves are still wet in the fingers. I wish we had our own bio-suits. The first twenty bags are okay; no virus, no disease of any kind. I can wipe down anything hard like a computer or digi display, but the other stuff has to go. Twenty-one has a cool pair of boots. They're not organic, so someone from Housewares can decide whether or not we should recycle them. Twenty-three – really? Did they think they could get a sandwich onto the outpost? It doesn't even look edible, truthfully, so I'm glad to get rid of it. PING! Now what? Virus alert. Everything this bag has touched gets quarantined. In the red box, seal the box, lock it in the orange SEARCH/DESTROY container. Twenty-four and Twenty-two have to be quarantined as well. Too bad for them.

It takes me five hours to get through all the stuff. Warren waits for me on the other side of the decon shower. He's too tall for his green suit. If he gets much taller, he'll have to transfer to a terra post. There the ceilings are three meters tall.

"Where've you been, Little Lacy?" he asks, smiling.

"Funny. We have ten extra people, y'know."

"Yes, I do," he says. "I'm still working with Housing, trying to find places for them."

"How about the next shuttle to 27?"

"27 isn't even fully operational; you know that."

"Better than paying emission taxes because I have to share quarters with someone."

"Did you find anything interesting?"

"Just a half-eaten sandwich - some kind of hash. One of the bags hit positive for a virus, but nothing outstanding."

"Too bad. I guess I'll stream something on my computer tonight."

"Where are you looking to put these kids?"

"I will do my best to stay out of your unit, if that's what you're asking," he tells me. I don't believe him for a second. "Are you going to dinner now?" he asks.

"Probably. You want me to wait for you?"

"No. I'll go after I finish with the newbies."

"Don't give me a cry-baby, Warren." He smiles as I head out to the main hall.

2.

Deck 17 is reserved for housing people. So is deck 4, but that's for officers and their families. Because I'm under 18, I still have to share our unit with thirteen other young people and a unit parent. Since I'm a Senior Grade 1, I only have to share my room with one other person. Until today. Two guys from Housing appear at my door with Gary, my unit parent. I pause the movie I'm streaming and take off my headphones.

"Hi, Lacy," Gary says with a smile.

"How many do I have?" I ask.

"Two for now. I know it's a lot,"

"I don't have to pay for them, do I? There's no way two more people are going to fit in here without going over the emissions max."

"That's not exactly true," one of the Housing guys says. "These rooms were built to accommodate four adults." Great, but I'm still only supposed to have one roommate.

Gary tries to be smooth. "It's only for a little while."

"Fine," I say. "Whatever." The grownups part ways to show two kids in yellow Under 16 suits. Their bedrolls and gear bags are bigger than they are. "Did you tell Jessie? She ought to know, too," I tell them.

"We'll let her know. In the meantime, you can figure out the details. Thank you very much, Lacy."

The new kids stay out of my room even after the old people go away. I put Jessie's and my stuff away. All our pictures above our desks go into our drawers.

"One of you can stay here on the desks. Just remember it's narrower than the regular bunks, and I guess one of you is stuck on the floor. If both of you are staying, we have to requisition two more bunks, but we don't have to worry about that now. I have the bottom one over here, and Jessie has the top." I slide open the left side closets. "You can hang your suits here, and we'll figure something out about any drawers. Try not to hyperventilate or get hysterical or you're going to have to pay an emissions tax."

"When do we get to eat?" the bigger one asks as she unrolls her mattress onto our desks.

"What happened to our stuff?" the other one starts with.

"Your biologicals were confiscated, and the rest will be brought to you here. As to food, you get to eat when you're not on shift or at school. Make sure you know how many credits you have, because if you go over, it's mostly bad stuff you have to do to earn those credits back. Did they give you your schedules yet?" The little one shakes her head. "What about your comm units?"

"They haven't given us anything except these bags and the bed," the bigger one tells me.

"All right. We'll see if they have you in the system yet. You need linens, credits, and a schedule. We have a communal terminal in the shared space; we can figure your stuff out there."

"Can we call home from here?" The little one is about to cry.

"When you get enough credits, you can call. Usually that takes a couple weeks, but we'll see what you get." Tears start sliding down her face. "Look; I know this is hard, but being here or on a terrapost is the best thing for you. You get to grow up, go to school, meet other people, and you don't catch the virus. I know you've seen what happens when people get the virus." She's quiet, but the tears flow even faster.

"Quit your whining," the big one sneers. "Just be glad someone paid your way out here."

"Let's go see what you've got." I direct them to our shared

space.

3.

Kira, the bigger of my new roommates, is sitting with a couple other new kids in Café 14C. They're already eating. I guess that's good; she won't be bugging me for every last little thing. I don't see the other one in the crowd. Not my problem. My problem is figuring out how I can get around paying the emissions tax for four people in my room. Actually, Jessie is older than I am; maybe she'll get hit with the fee instead.

"Hello?" I snap to attention. "What do you want for dinner?" the server barks.

"Soup, sandwich, and beans." They get dropped on a tray, and the tray is shoved to the next section. "Are those real apples?" I ask.

"Grown right here on post 16. Get 'em while you can."

"I'll take two." On my tray, and the tray is shoved to the register. Grab a bottle of juice, scan my ID, find someplace to sit.

"Lacy!" I sit with Jessie at a nearby table. She has a few apples as well. "I figure we can sell them in a couple days after food service runs out," she says.

"No, thanks. I'd rather eat mine. How'd you get a break now?"

"It's time for our annual OEV training. Don't you read your messages? Come on, Lacy."

"I thought it was more junk mail. Sorry." I hate Old Earth Virus training, especially after a meal. I wonder if

"Tomorrow morning's all full," Jessie says, reading my mind. "Tonight's your last chance to avoid remediation." I hate when she does that. Better that happens, though, than I go through the whole class again.

"Do you know where our little roommate is?" I ask Jessie.

"Probably sitting in the unit wasting our air. Why? You're not getting me to pay for her, Lacy. No way."

"You're the oldest one in the room."

"You're the Senior 1; you make the most credits," she counters. "Maybe she'll get sent to a different post."

"Somebody has to," I tell her. "We have ten extra people right now."

"Great. I'm still not paying for a cry-baby."

"Then how about the other one; Kira?"

"Let's see how much they go over, and then we'll talk."

4.

The bleeding alone makes me not want to catch OEV, but then they have to show the rest of the clip. I hate that the dead people look like the soup we just had for dinner.

"This is why we do not allow biologicals onto the outpost," the video drones on. "One micron of this virus can replicate and create havoc in under 24 weeks." I guess it's good we have to watch this every year – just in case people forget what it looks like when you're dying. I don't know how healthy kids are born on Old Earth. I do know they get sick pretty quickly if they're not vaccinated. My parents couldn't afford to keep getting us all shots, so they chose four of us. I guess I'm glad they sent me away pretty soon after my second set.

"Does anyone have any questions?" breaks my daydreaming. "You in the back." I sit up, hoping the instructor's not calling on me. I hate pop quizzes. I really should've listened more to the lecture. He points this way. "Yeah, you. Smack that kid next to you." I hit the sleeping child. She falls out of her seat, but at least she's awake now. The man talks some more about hand washing, personal hygiene, don't take anything that looks biological if it didn't come from the station.

Now we have a short test. Twenty questions that determine whether you keep your job or go through remediation. I don't want to go through remediation again. They can throw you off the outpost if you do it too many times. Blainey says they'd send you back to Old Earth, but I don't really believe her. She makes up a lot of stories to make the new people think she's important. BEEP! No remediation for me – I got a 90%. Not so lucky is the girl who was sleeping. She gets a low, long tone. Not my problem. My problem is my little roommate. She got sick watching the video, and she's still crying so badly, she hasn't taken the test yet.

"Ten minutes to finish the test, or you automatically go to remediation." The girl starts bawling, so I go to comfort her.

"Look; it's not that bad," I tell her. "All that video shows is what could happen, okay? Most people live ten, twenty years with the stuff and die of old age." That made it worse. "Kid, it's okay. You're safe now. That's why your parents sent you here."

"My parents died when I was little," she sobs. "This is what happened to them. I know it."

"Okay, but you need to take the test. If you think this video was bad, just wait and see what remediation looks like."

Jessie joins us from the middle of the room. "Kid, if you don't stop crying, they're going to send you back. Is that what you want?" The little girl pauses for a moment. "Nobody wants you to go, but if you can't follow directions, if you can't stop crying, you can't stay here."

"I could get sent back? Really? That would be cool." She wipes her eyes and nose.

"Why would you want to go back to a place where you're just going to die like that?" Jessie demands.

"I get to see my granddad and grandmom one more time before ...." She looks as if she's going to bawl again, but she doesn't.

"You want to waste the money and hours and resources everyone spent to get you up here? You're either really brave or really stupid, little girl." To me, Jessie says, "Good luck with this one. I'm done." And she walks away.

"Come on, kid. Take the test." I think she's going to do it. "It's only twenty questions." She doesn't appear to be dumb, but then she starts howling at the top of her lungs. She starts

coughing, and I wonder if she's going to get sick again. Everyone

else finishes their tests while Security comes and takes the little girl

to another area. That's the last I see of her.

5.

Loading Dock 18C-211 is as clean as it's going to get. What really needs to happen is Housekeeping needs to come paint over the scrub marks and where the blue primer shows through. My comm beeps once. Report to hydroponics 3A. I've never been in as far as the third deck before. Hope my clearance is okay. The last time I worked in Sector A, an Earth Executive had come to visit. At least I have something to do besides wiping down the docking bays one more time. Change into my regular blue suit and head out.

"Where to, Little Lacy?" Warren's at the checkpoint before we enter the commercial zone on 18B.

"Nowhere. What's it to you?"

"What?" he laughs. "Am I getting an attitude from you?"

"You bet, especially when you're just being nosy. I know you know where I'm going."

"Keep your eyes open, okay? I want a full report on what you find in there."

"You know it's all classified stuff. I couldn't tell you if I wanted to."

"C'mon, Lacy. What's a good secret among friends?" I roll my eyes, and he sits back at his desk. He may be older, but I still outrank him.

Swipe my ID at the elevator control panel, and the third deck button lights up. Nobody else gets on until the sixth deck. A blue suit like mine, but he has an engineering patch on it, no stripes on his sleeves. His ID lights up the second deck button - command and control. He doesn't look that important, but maybe he's off duty. BING! Third deck.

The door opens to a bright white hallway. The hiss of the door closing is startling. I'd hate to be housekeeping for this level. No sound from the vents, nothing at all except my boots on the floor. About seventy meters ahead is a sector break. There's no security person, but I do need to swipe my ID again. The door to Sector A opens without a sound.

"You're early," someone says from behind a control center. The bays with plants are huge. The plants don't look like anything I've seen before, even in books. Some of the trees look as if they have tiger stripes on them. I had no idea the station would hold stuff this big. "Let me see your ID." The woman in a white suit scans my card but still isn't happy. "How did you get to be a Senior Grade 1? Never mind. How much can you lift?" I'm pretty sure I don't like this person.

"About thirty kilos without help." No identifying patches or stripes on her suit. What is going on in here? Is this a set-up?

"That'll do," she says. "I'm sorry. I thought they were sending someone more experienced. Oh well. So, we have four bays that need clearing and decontamination, bays M through P. Do you understand what that entails?"

It means a lot of junk going into bags that go into decon boxes, and the fluids go in giant vats. "Yes, ma'am. Do you have all the equipment, or do I need to get mine?" I ask.

"We have everything you need. It's all in the shed by bay P. Don't let any of the fungus touch you. It tends to burn."

She goes back to her control center, and I go to the decon "shed." It's bigger than any I've seen before, but this is deck 3. They pretty much get what they want. I wonder if the chief knows about the burning fungus. I wonder if the station master knows what goes on in here. The bio suit smells new, as if nobody else has even tried it on, and it's a couple sizes too big. Better that than too small. I'll need medium gloves to go over the suit.

Five hours of work, and it looks as if I haven't done a thing. I hope they'll still pay me for what I have done. I'm on my third pair of gloves because the brownish fungus truly eats almost anything it touches. At least there's four or five more pairs in the decon shed. I bet if I stretched the roots from the host plants, we'd reach into the next solar system.

"Excuse me," comes through my suit. I jump at how loud it is compared to the sound of my breathing. "Excuse me, you need to prepare to leave now."

Close up the bag I'm working on, drop it in the decon box, drop the box into the large container at the end of the bed. I guess I did some work – I can see the fluid on part of bay M. The supply room has its own shower and changing room, but it's not like the loading docks. There's no separate air lock between the shower and the changing room, and there aren't windows in the shower here.

When I'm finished cleaning up, the woman comes out of the control room. "Can you work the rest of the week?" she asks. She has a tablet in her hand.

"Sure," I say. "We'll need to arrange for all the container pickups, and vats for the"

"I'll take care of that," she snaps. "If you can clear these bays in the next five days, how about we double your salary?"

"Not a problem," I almost smile. I hope she doesn't count that against me, the smiling.

"Thank you. That will be all for today."

"Thanks."

She types something into her tablet then goes back to her control room. All this digging and moving has made me hungry.

6.

It's pretty easy to get a seat here in Cafe 14C at this hour, but Kira slides in next to me with her tray of food. How'd she get enough credits for meat?

"Did you really work on the third deck?" she asks quietly.

"What do you know about that?" I finish my first sandwich in three bites.

"I know the third shift station master was pissed you got the job."

"Third shift is a bunch of lightweights," I tell her. "They get upset all the time when we remind them. The only S1s on third shift were transferred there when we got a new Commander."

"So?" she presses.

Let's change the subject. "So how'd you get enough credits for all that food? Your parents make a donation?"

"I work in IT. You want a raise?"

"I'm already an S1, thanks."

"Yeah, but you're not due 'til you're twenty one. Sure you can wait that long?"

"Why would I get a raise now?" I don't need any bosses coming down on me if she screws things up. I'm almost due a two week vacation. I don't need that taken away because of something stupid.

"Why did they send you to deck three?" she asks.

"Fine," I tell her. A few more credits won't be so bad. "But it's your head if you get caught."

"Please. The only way I got caught on Old Earth was my stupid cousin blabbed he had an endless supply of diesel. If he'd kept his mouth shut, we all could've gotten to a terrapost further away than this place."

"You had enough money to go to a terrapost?"

"Yeah, for eight people. I was so pissed when I had to give half of it back." She's a funny kid. I wouldn't have thought to do something like that. "You didn't really think I'd be dumb enough to return it all, do you?"

"Sucks you can't touch it for a long time."

"It's okay. My probation only lasts 'til I'm thirty. I'll be free and clear and rich all at the same time. Here." Kira passes me a sandwich with real meat in it instead of protein hash. "This one's free." I might get to like her after all.

7.

The learning lab on 15D is full of people cramming for exams. We're all quiet, so the security officer doesn't have to work that hard. At the pace I'm going, I'll be finished with my classwork in another month. I want to get into a Forensic Science course, but Warren says you have to be over 18 to be assigned one of those. In the meantime it's algebra, anatomy, microbiology, and ancient texts. My digi screen suddenly stops playing the digestive system. I look up, see Warren messing around again.

"That's gross, Lacy," he proclaims. "Why are you even looking at this?"

"Don't you have a docking bay to patrol?" I set the lesson back to the beginning.

"You're so not funny," he laughs, sitting next to me. "How was work today?"

"It's fine. They're paying me a lot of money to clean up after the mad scientists. No big deal."

"Are you kidding? How many people do you know who went that far into the station?"

"It's nothing, Warren. Well, except it's all white down there."

"So are the decon stations. You're really not going to tell me anything?"

"Sorry, but there's nothing to say. You want to watch a movie later?"

"I'm going swimming, then I'm going to sleep. Guess who drew dawn patrol the next two weeks?" Artificial dawn is at 0500.

"Sucks to be you then."

He gets up to go. "That stuff is still disgusting." He makes it out before the security officer gets upset.

8.

I really hope I can finish this movie before someone comes into the room. No such luck. A knock at the door, then Jessie steps in.

"Hey, roomie." She jumps into her bunk and bangs her head on the ceiling. "Damn it!"

"Are you bleeding?" I ask, pausing my video.

"No, but it still hurts. What's new with our little one? Although, she's not so little, is she?"

"She's all right, Jessie. She works in IT."

"I heard she's an S2 already."

"She's only 14."

"Still, she's got to be pretty smart if they brought her all the way out here."

"There's no room before Outpost 12."

"There's always room on the terraposts. Whatcha watching?"

"*Lost In Space*. The original was done on film."

"Film film or digital?"

"It said analog film. It's pretty funny."

"You don't get tired of space junk?"

"It's all right."

"Well, when I get enough credits, I'm moving to Terra 12. Supposedly, they have a rec center there, and they're able to hold 100,000 regulars."

"Where did you hear they're building a post for 100,000 people? C'mon, Jess."

"It doesn't matter. At least there you could go outside and breathe some fresh air or eat something that wasn't 3-D printed for you. You can come if you want."

"Maybe I will."

"Maybe you should pay my way; then we'll be even for me taking care of you on this ship."

"Yeah, whatever." I plug my headphones in and turn the movie back on. I'm going to miss Jessie when she goes to a singles unit next year.

9.

So far so good – my ID still lights up the third deck button. Nobody else gets on this time. Straight through the sector break, straight to the decon shed to change. The lady stays in her control room. She doesn't say anything as I get to work. No more fungus on the plants means I can get these beds cleared by the end of the day instead of the end of the week. Maybe I'll get a couple extra days off after this.

"Hello?" comes through the decon suit. It's not the woman who hired me.

"Yes, sir."

"We need you to take samples of the materials before they're destroyed."

"Does that include the things already in bags?"

"I'm afraid so. We'll pay you for an additional two days, of course." Of course.

"No problem," I tell him. At least I'll eat well next week. I could put some credits away towards my vacation, too.

There's a lot to sample. I try to get the stuff that hasn't been contaminated by other stuff, but it's kind of hard now that most of it is in plastic bags. I wonder what this fungus looks like under the microscope. I save some in an extra glass vial and put it in my pocket.

10.

SEE YOU @ 1800 is Warren's answer to my beep. Thirty minutes late, he saunters into the learning lab on 16C. There are a couple other students sitting close to the security officer by the front door. I'm in the last seat in the last row, listening to Chekhov in Russian. I don't know why we bother since English is the official human language.

"Hey," he says quietly. I stop the player. "How go the dead languages?"

"They're not quite dead yet," I tell him. "What took you so long?"

"I had to finish a report."

"What, some juniors from G sector fighting again?"

"A couple old timers who should know better. I think they're getting shipped off the outpost. So what's up? What'd you find?" I slide the glass vial from my pocket. "This looks cool. What is it?"

"Some fungus thing they're growing on 3A. It doesn't seem to eat through glass, but it tears up just about everything else."

He looks carefully at the specimen. "You always find the neat stuff. Do they know you took this?"

"What, am I stupid? C'mon, Warren."

"I'll call you when I can get into the lab."

"You think Idris would like this?" Idris is Warren's friend. He's really good at getting people out of trouble, but you usually owe him huge favors after he does that for you. I currently owe him two favors. He also likes a good mystery, so this might be perfect for him.

"Maybe," Warren says. "Maybe we'll keep this for ourselves."

"Once you figure out what it is." Warren puts the vial up his sleeve then heads out.

11.

There's something new on my digi screen. I know I didn't order these movies. Actually, I don't really care right now. All I want is to go to sleep. Except Kira's in her bunk, watching something. I wish she'd use headphones all the time, not just in public. She pauses her video.

"Hey. Are you staying up?" she asks.

"Nope. I don't know where Jessie is, but I'm going to sleep." She gets her headphones out. "Not for nothing, but did you hack my entertainment account?"

"No. I just thought you might like some of the stuff I have on file."

"What archives did you access? The really old ones are on film. I don't have money for"

"Nobody was harmed in the downloading of these videos, okay? And these were free, just so you know. Remember, the only way I got caught on Old Earth was that people talked too much. You certainly don't have that problem."

"So you collect old videos?"

"I used to. Then they started taking up too much memory. I stopped at the 2200s."

I shouldn't ask her, but "Hey, can you hack the lab computers on 15 and 16?"

"For a fee."

"Really?"

"I had enough money to go to Terra 8, Lacy. How do you think that happened?"

"How much would it be?"

"The hack or Terra 8?"

"Terra 8 is about 100,000 credits from here."

"It depends on how complicated the security is and how classified the material is," she says. "Why? Wouldn't you rather know about deck 3?"

"I guess."

"I bet it'd be more interesting. What have you learned already?"

"Nothing yet," I tell her. "I don't even know who's running the program there."

"But you could find out."

"So could you, apparently."

"So I could." She puts her headphones on, and I get under my covers.

12.

Where Warren gets the codes to open doors on this station, I'll never know. It's probably safer that way. It's good I took a nap this afternoon. We're in an analysis lab on 15C tonight way past our bedtimes. He's looking at the fungus I gave him under the microscope.

"Is there more of this stuff?" he asks without looking up.

"I don't know."

"Did they send it to recycling while you were working there?"

"All they had me do was put it in decon boxes. They said they'd do the rest."

"I'll bet they're saving it for something." He opens a blue vial and puts a drop on the slide. "Look at this. This is great!" Warren moves so I can look in the eyepiece. All I see is tan stuff surrounding the blue stuff and then the blue stuff disappearing. "Isn't that cool?" he asks.

"What is that, starch or something?"

"It's starch. The fungus is eating it. It's eating the whole cell."

"Is that good?" I wonder.

"Maybe they could use it to clean the food printers. I wonder what they're going to do with this." He puts the fungus sample back in the glass tube and the slide into the dirty glass container.

I should know better, but "So what're you going to do with it?" Warren has a collection of stuff he keeps safe in his lock box.

"Oh, I don't know. I'll think of something. Why? Do you have anything in mind?"

"No. And anyway, there are too many little people in my unit for me to keep it."

"We need to go, though. Third shift cleaners are coming soon." He logs us out of the lab then takes both sets of our gloves. I don't know what he does with them to avoid the DNA scans in the waste recycler. I guess the less I know the better.

13.

Four clangs in a row, a second of silence, then four more loud noises and the emergency lights come on. 0312. This better be a safety drill. Five more sets of ringing at full volume.

"What the hell?" Kira mutters as she falls out of bed. Jessie already has her suit and boots on before I can clear my head.

"Something's wrong," I tell Kira.

"Really? I didn't know."

"Shut up, both of you," Jessie whispers.

This is a general alarm, so we stay in our room 'til we get further instructions. We finish getting dressed in silence. We'd know by now if there was a breach somewhere. Maybe the air scrubbers are failing again.

"Jessie,"

"I don't know," she says quietly.

Kira gets her computer out just in time for the Commander's face to appear dead center on the screen. "Attention all personnel. This is not a drill. I repeat, this is not a drill." Just in case we didn't have a digi screen, the announcement is coming through our comm units as well. "We will be conducting an outpost-wide decontamination starting right now. All personnel are confined to quarters or are to hold in place. There are no exceptions." The monitor clicks off.

"Lacy, what's going on?" Jessie asks.

"I don't know. Nothing's come on board while I was working."

"Could it be from another shift?"

"It would've had to have come from a ship, and the only thing that docked here since the kids came aboard was from Terra 5."

"Let's see what Gary has to say," Jessie suggests.

We open our door to find the rest of our unit in the common area. Gary and his son, John, are here as well. Our younger kids are clearly upset.

"What does this mean?" Blainey asks.

"We stay here 'til they clean the whole outpost," Gary explains. "It's going to take a while, so we should just relax. You can go back to sleep if you want."

"So it's true," John says.

"What's true?"

"I heard that call you got, dad. They said the virus got onto an outpost."

Gary hugs his son. "No, that's not exactly true. At least, they're not sure that's what happened."

"Yes, it is," Kira says quietly. "All the station masters got a notice that Outpost 8 is infected."

"How did you hear that?" Gary asks.

"First shift doesn't use his earpiece when he's in his office, so the people who work there can hear everything he does."

"How could the decon units miss something?" I ask. "We've been doing this for a hundred years. There are protocols that stop this from happening."

"I don't know," Gary says. "They gave some of us a heads up that there may be a problem, but I don't know."

"Does this mean we're infected?" his son asks.

"I don't know. Let's not worry just yet, okay? Lacy, you work in decon. Have we ever had an infection pass through quarantine?"

"No way. We know what we're doing."

"Okay then. Let's just wait 'til they come to clean us up." I don't know about anyone else, but I'm going back to sleep.

14.

0715. "What else do you have on your computer?" Jessie asks Kira. They're huddled together on Kira's bunk, staring at Kira's digi screen. There's no sense in trying to sleep now, especially if we're going to be locked up in here for a while. "How do you keep that thing working anyway?"

"It's not that hard," Kira says. "I used to have someone at a recycling plant who'd supply everything I needed, but he's stuck on Old Earth."

"How'd you pay him? None of this old stuff is cheap."

"I made sure life was comfortable for him and his family. Do you want a movie or TV?"

"I have a mini projector," I tell them. "We could show it on the wall."

"I thought you were asleep," Jessie says.

"We didn't mean to wake you," Kira adds.

"Yeah, well, who can sleep through this anyway, right?"

"Lacy, when was the last time we had to quarantine someone here?" Jessie asks.

"Just the once when the scanners malfunctioned. I don't think any station past outpost 4 has ever had real problems. That's why the protocols went into place ninety years ago. That's why they scan people on Earth before they ever get anywhere."

"It's still not foolproof," Kira tells us. "There were twelve kids taken off the line before we came here." We would've run out of air for sure if sixty-two kids had come to this station.

"I guess it's time to develop the next round of vaccine then," I say. "Do you want the projector?"

"Is it in your drawer?"

"Bottom left." Jessie gets the machine. "What're we watching?"

"I don't really care," Kira says, hooking up the projector. "I've watched everything a hundred times already. How about old *Star Trek*? I have the original series."

"The first original series? No way." Jessie is too enthusiastic for this time of the morning.

"I have Mars Colony Productions, too. They can be a little gross, though." The Mars colony put out some horror shows before it became the home of the Central Control. It's funny that the Earth Executive spends most of his time on Mars.

"Do you have '*My Favorite Martian*'?" Jessie asks.

"Old or ancient?"

"The old ones - the ones from Mars." Kira pushes some buttons, and Jessie shines the projector onto the door.

15.

I'm tired of watching movies, I'm tired of playing video games. I'm tired of being cooped up with a bunch of little ones. I'm all caught up with my schoolwork, even ahead in algebra. No place to go, nothing to do. John is pretty good at UNO. He's beating Blainey and Scott every game.

"And we switch directions again, which means it's your turn," John says to the young boy on his right.

"How am I supposed to get rid of any of these cards?" Scott whines.

"Play right, and you, too, can win," John chuckles. The little one plays a blue 2. Gary comes out of his quarters. He's holding a stuffed dog.

"John, do you have everything you need from here?" he asks.

"Hold on, dad; I'm winning."

"They're decontaminating our quarters. Do you have everything you want?"

"Oh. I need to get -" John sees the stuffed dog. "Never mind. Thanks, dad." Gary closes and seals the door to their living space then taps a message on his comm unit. It beeps once, and Gary sits with the kids at the small table.

"Why are they cleaning your place first?" Blainey asks.

"I think that's where we're going once they've decontaminated us," Gary responds. "Who's winning?"

"Who do you think? At least we're not betting money." I guess I'll go listen to another podcast.

Two hours into Music From The 2100s, our section master comes on our comms and digi screens. "Attention, unit dwellers. You are next to be decontaminated. In a moment or two, you will receive further instructions on how to proceed. If you are unable or unwilling to comply, you will suffer the consequences." The digi screens go off. The sprays and scrubbing aren't all bad, but I hate other people doing it for me. I think I know how to wash myself, thanks.

"Who gets to go first?" Blainey asks Gary.

"I think it should go in rank order," Jessie says. Jessie does that to remind Blainey she's still a J2 trainee. I heard Blainey only got promoted because her boss didn't want to listen to her anymore.

"I think it should go according to longevity," Blainey counters. She would - she's been here almost as long as Gary has.

"We'll go oldest to youngest," Gary says. That means Jessie goes after Gary.

"Attention unit dwellers," comes over the comms. "Prepare for cleansing. Remove all articles except your suit, underwear, and boots. This includes your glasses and comm units. You will, one by one, leave out your front door and follow the directions you are given. First in line, please proceed."

Gary takes off his jewelry and comm unit. The door to the main hall opens. They've set up a portable decon station in the hall. After Gary goes through the door, it closes. Two more people ahead of me.

It's cold in the shower. That makes the scrubbing even worse than usual. Rinse, scrub again, rinse twice more, dry off. At least I get a new suit and new boots out of this. I'll have to get another decon patch for this suit. The clean side of the tent does open into Gary's quarters.

"Nice place," I tell him. Two sleeping rooms, a kitchenette in the common area, and a private bathroom. I wonder where he got all the travel posters from Old Earth. I didn't know he was into ancient history.

"It's not bad," Gary tells us. "It's designed for a couple with four kids."

"That would make this really crowded, wouldn't it?"

"No more so than the rest of the unit," Gary says.

"Do you think they're going to charge us for the new stuff?" Jessie asks. "I can clean my own clothes without losing credits."

"We could sell them our old things, make it an even trade," I suggest.

"I'm guessing it'll work out in the end," Gary says. "We can ask Kira when she gets here."

16.

Sixteen people in a space built for six isn't much fun. Blainey's been going on about ancient Earth history and all the stories she read about stuff in pre-history. I don't know how much of her blathering is true. I don't really care.

"There was a time when all there was was posters and pictures on paper," she continues.

"No way," one of the little ones says. "You're just making that up."

"I'm serious. Moving pictures didn't start 'til the early 1900s, right, Gary?"

"That's true," he tells them. "And then it was only in black and white. Color wasn't mainstream 'til the second half of the 1900s." Gary's digi screen beeps. No face comes on the video part, but we all hear "Attention unit dwellers. You may now return to your unit. You are still confined to quarters until further notice."

Gary unlocks and slowly opens the door to our unit. The vent hasn't cleared the sour smell of disinfectant. At least it's not greasy like the stuff we use on the docking bays. The little ones rush to collect their things from the middle of the floor.

"No, that's my comm unit," Scott grumbles.

"No, you're 18507, I'm 18705," John tells him. "See? I still have the orange sticker for Under 12 on mine."

"Where's my stuff?" another child whines. "Gary, I can't find oh, never mind."

I go to my room to find Jessie and Kira putting their things away. Mine are all on the floor, including my lock box.

"They didn't take the closets apart," Jessie reports. "They just sprayed everything they could see." I put my pictures and stuff in my desk drawers.

"All your things are okay?" I ask. It doesn't look as if anything was confiscated from my lock box.

"All accounted for," Kira says. "I don't know what the disinfectant does to the old world tech, but it's all here." Kira looks in my box. "That's a cool watch. Does it still work?"

I shake it a little, and it starts ticking. "Looks that way. You have to shake it for something like five minutes for it to work all day."

"How'd you get it past security?"

"It's not organic. My dad gave it to me before we left."

"I'm going to wash all my stuff tonight," Jessie tells us.
"You can run your suits and things with mine if you want."

"Won't it cost money to do a large load?" Kira asks.

"You'll just owe me a favor," Jessie smiles. Her favors are
usually little things that a couple credits can fix. Jessie learned how
to do laundry right when she started working for housekeeping.
Sometimes it's worth paying someone else to do it for you.

17.

We're not supposed to waste food, but I'm not sure how many of these emergency rations I can take. Never mind this batch was supposed to be recycled two years ago. I wonder what the food printers can do with sustenance bars. We were decontaminated two days ago, and yet, we wait.

"Gin!" one of the little kids howls. The others playing with her drop their cards in a pile.

"Gary, why don't we have our own food printers?" Scott complains.

"What would we use to make food from?" Kira shoots back. She hasn't been off her computer since we were decontaminated.

"Anything's better than this crap."

"It takes too much room and too many supplies for each unit to feed themselves," Gary explains. "Anyway, it won't be very long before they let us loose."

"The decon's finished," Kira says, clearing the screen on her tablet.

"How do you know?" Scott sneers. "What're you, a spy or something?"

"Why would you know if she was a spy?" Blainey asks.

"Shutup, Blainey. I'm not stupid. Where'd she get all this tech stuff in the first place?"

"Maybe you're the spy, asking all these questions," Kira tells him.

"Maybe you brought the virus with you," Scott continues. Our comms beep. Even the smallest child is quiet as the Commander's face appears on the digi screens.

"Attention all personnel, this is not a drill. I repeat, this is not a drill. The decontamination of this station is complete. I want to personally thank each person on this outpost for their cooperation, their patience, and their understanding. In just under two hours, at 1300 hours, we will return to our normal activities. Until then, everyone should stay where they are. Food service will be operational at all locations by 2000 hours. Any questions should be directed to your section chief or unit parent. That is all for now." And the screens go blank.

"We still can't eat real food? Is that man crazy?" a little one cries.

"I'm sure the main cafeterias will be open before 2000," Gary reassures us. "The good news is we're all clear."

"For now," Scott grumbles.

"I bet there's going to be a whole lot of new regulations," Blainey proclaims. "They're probably going to take all our stuff, not just the organics."

"If that were true, Blainey, they would've done it already," I say. "Besides, we're not the ones in trouble."

"Dad, what did they do with Outpost 8?" John asks.

"I don't know," Gary responds. "I'm sure they'll tell us soon." I'll ask Kira about that later, when we're alone.

18.

"Not interested." Idris continues to clean the food service trays. I don't know why I have to be here, but Warren insisted.

"C'mon, buddy," Warren says smoothly. "You really should see this."

"Nothing you have in your pocket will return the favors you owe me."

"First, I only owe you one favor, and second, this stuff is sick."

"First, what do you call making sure your girlfriend here didn't run out of credits? I had to deal with human waste for that one. Pass me those things."

"I'm not his girlfriend," I tell them. Warren slides the dirty trays to Idris.

"And what you did is between you and her," Warren says, "but I get it, Idris. You're not interested in a mystery. You're too busy."

"Stop trying to push my buttons, Junior Patrolman. It won't work."

"No, that's cool. We'll just figure it out ourselves. You missed a tray."

"Did not." We turn to leave. "Oh, all right. Fine, Warren. What do you have that's so fascinating?" Warren gives him a vial of the fungus from 3A. "Who else knows about this?"

"Just us and the scientists growing the stuff on deck 3."

"Third deck?" Idris is definitely interested now.

"3A to be specific," I point out.

"Why didn't they confiscate it during the decontamination?"

"I have a special place nobody else knows about," Warren smiles. "We'll see you later?"

"Yeah. I'll beep you." Idris slides the vial into his pocket then gets the next stack of trays.

19.

"Bay doors closed, pressurization complete," the computer says calmly. Looking at the flight manifest, there's only one person on the transport besides the pilots. He must be pretty important. At least they brought more supplies for the food printers. Warren and the security chief are watching the unloading process.

"What's taking so long?" I ask.

"He probably doesn't want to go through security," Warren suggests. Sure enough, a fat man comes out with five bags of luggage. He's not even wearing a regular suit. He must be really important if he's allowed to carry all that stuff. I can't hear what he's saying, but it takes a long time for the pilots to show him to the locker room.

The automated recording again: "Please leave your bags outside the door; they will be taken to your quarters shortly. Please step into the" blah blah blah.

As they disappear into the locker room, Warren smiles, "Suit up, kid. Time to go to work."

Food elements. 3-D printer heads. Junior pilot's bag. Senior pilot's bag. All according to regulation. Now to the passenger's stuff. What is this man thinking? Does he really believe we're that stupid? He must've been on a terrapost all his life. All the clothes have to go, as does the leather briefcase. Keep the stuff inside the briefcase, we can always wipe them down. PING. What now? My sensors are still half charged. PING. Not my comm. Not the speakers here in decon. The tool box. It's not reading anything we usually test for. Maybe he didn't wash it out right. Maybe. Or wait. There's a cover to something in the bottom of the tool box. I should just quarantine the whole load of bags, but curiosity gets the best of me.

20.

Warren finally shows up twenty minutes after I beep him. He's smiling for some stupid reason.

"What's up, Little Lacy? Find anything good?"

"Warren, you said I could trust you with anything, right?" I start with.

"Sure. What's up? This jerk sure has a lot of crap with him, doesn't he? How'd you get through it so fast?"

"You said no matter what, I should come to you, right?"

"Lacy, c'mon; what'd you find, a Twinkie?" Count on Warren to remind you of your most favorite OE treat. I haven't had one in I don't know how long. "If you did, let me have it?" he asks. "You know Idris loves them, and he's been kind of cranky lately,"

"No. It's not like that, Warren. Promise you won't say anything?"

"Lacy, what did you find?" I show him the vacutainer. Warren's face goes all serious. "What is that?" The only other time I've seen vacutainers is when they work with people's fluids in the lab. This one has a thin, green liquid in it.

"I don't know, but here."

"Where did you find this?"

"It was in his tool kit under a false bottom. I almost didn't find it. It doesn't register as anything we know, but this is a vacutainer, right?" Warren takes it from me and slides it up his sleeve. "That is what this is, right?"

"Shutup, Lacy, please." I haven't seen Warren this upset since the five kids were quarantined in my training years. Turned out the scanner was broken then, but it sure woke people up that week. "Listen. Don't say anything to anyone about this, okay?"

"What, am I stupid?"

"Report the false bottom, but you didn't find anything there. Got it?"

"Sure. Thanks, Warren."

"No problem. Give me a couple days to figure out what's going on."

I smile politely, and we head our separate ways. My comm beeps -- my boss wants to see me. The fat man from the shuttle has some questions.

21.

I can hear the visitor yelling at the section chief through the hall doors. The Earth man's face is red all the way up to the bald spot on top of his head, and he's wearing an officer's bathrobe. The section chief sees me through the door and waves at me.

"Decon Specialist Lacy Harrison, sir." I stand as tall as I can. Both men are a good head and shoulders taller than me. The fat man laughs.

"This is the person that destroyed my belongings?" he roars.

"The only things that were destroyed were foreign biologicals," the section chief says smoothly.

"Says who?"

"Says the technician on duty."

"Obviously your technician is mistaken then," the Earth man announces. "Now to the matter of compensation."

"There will be no compensation for illegal materials brought onto the outpost. The only business at hand is determining whether or not you knowingly brought said items."

"Why would I bring a virus here?"

"Is that what you did? Harrison, did you find a virus among our visitor's things?"

"There was an undetermined residue in the toolbox, sir."

"'Undetermined residue,' how ridiculous. That makes absolutely no sense. What does make sense is you're afraid of me, so you do what you can to sabotage my work." He looks at me. "How old are you?"

"Her age is none of your concern," the section chief says.

"I mean, really; how much schooling could you have had before you started working here? Three years, four? Can she even read?"

"Her schooling is irrelevant, and my specialist is a Senior Grade 1. Not that that is your business."

"Everything that goes on at this station is my business, Chief. You'd best remember that."

"You'd best remember that you are a guest of ours at the request of the Earth Executive." The section chief looks at me. "You can go back to work now." I must've looked nervous because he smiles. "You're fine. Just do your job."

"Yes, sir," I tell him, maybe a little too enthusiastically. That includes destroying the fat man's clothes. He'll have to squeeze into a regulation suit after all.

22.

Warren and I are in an analysis lab on 15C. He's looking at the makeup of the stuff I found in the Earth man's bag.

"Look at this," Warren says, standing up straight. I look into the microscope and see a bunch of weird shapes and colors.

"What am I looking for?" I ask.

"The one on the right is the OE Virus. The one on the left is the investigator's stuff."

"They don't look anything alike."

"That's my point. This is something new."

"How do you know? You're a junior security patrol specialist."

"I read things," he says. What he's really saying is I shouldn't ask him any more questions.

"Maybe Idris can help us with this?" I ask.

"Maybe."

"Maybe we should go to the section master with this, Warren. He'd know what to do for sure."

"We don't know if he's in on it, Lacy. Think about it. If the Earth Executive sent this man here with all his stuff, it could be big trouble; huge."

"But the section master is our boss. We should tell our boss what we've found."

"We'll tell Idris," Warren says after a while, "but we can't say anything to anyone else. Got it?"

"Sure, but"

"No buts. You have to stay quiet 'til we know what we have."

"What do you think we have, Warren?"

"I don't know, but it looks bad."

23.

Kira comes into our room and closes the door. I turn my music up, but she sits next to me anyway. She waits 'til I take my headphones off.

"What's up?" I try to smile.

"You might want to tell your friend to stick to using the lab during third shift."

"Excuse me?"

"What's his name, Warren? They're cracking down on illegal pass codes with that guy from Old Earth here. I really don't want you guys getting sent somewhere because a junior security patrolman or a decon specialist got caught where they didn't belong."

"I will certainly pass that along. Thanks." I put my headphones on, but she doesn't move. "What?"

"That's the question, isn't it? Whatever you guys found?"

"I don't know what you're talking about."

"Come on, Lacy. That fat man can't be all pissed off just because you incinerated his clothes."

"He had a nice leather briefcase that had to go."

"And what was in that case? Or was it in one of the boxes he said had tools in it?"

"I still don't know what you're talking about."

"Really? You guys were just looking at an empty slide under a power microscope?"

I wonder who else saw the video feed. "Why are you so interested in all this? You're just an IT trainee."

"Please. I'm waiting for the day IT teaches me something new."

"Can't help you there," I tell her.

"If something big was about to happen, you'd tell us, wouldn't you? You're not going to just let us find out from the station master, right?"

"Kira, you need to stop with all this mystery crap. There's no big plot or scheme or anything."

"Then what is that man doing here?"

24.

My comm beeps once. Time to meet the guys. Kira's still watching a movie or something on her digi screen.

"Can you keep a secret?" I ask her. She takes off her headphones.

"You're kidding, right? Is this about the fat man? Did he bring something illegal on board?"

"You need to be quiet, Kira, or nothing good will come of this."

"Sure. Not a problem. When are we going?"

"Now. C'mon." We get our boots on and head to C sector. Warren meets us at the sector break.

"Why'd you bring her?" Warren asks.

"She figured things out. Where are we going?"

"14D recycler. Let's go." In three decks, around to sector D.

"So why are we meeting in a recycling center?" I ask Warren. I don't know how people work in here. It all smells like human waste to me.

"Do you know anywhere else where they don't have cameras every five meters?" Kira replies.

"And since nobody comes in here for no reason," Warren explains, "we're just looking for a ring that got washed away in a sink or something." I'm really not sure this is a good idea.

Warren flashes a different badge at the door to the recycling center control room. A moment, then the door opens. Idris is at the first computer next to the door. He's the only one in this room.

"So we're looking for a ring," Warren starts. Idris closes the door behind us.

"What'd you bring her for?" Idris demands, looking at Kira.

"She knows," I say.

"She knows shit," Idris sneers. "You all just go home; I'll handle this myself."

"The hell you are," Kira tells him. "One call to the section chief, we're all off the outpost. I'm sure that's really what you want, right?" Idris is super mad now. "Look; I don't care what's in the tube. I just know something bad is about to happen, and I want to get ahead of it."

"What's your job?"

"Programmer," she says.

"Can you get into the system here?" Idris asks.

"How do you think people got those extra credits?"

He thinks for a minute. "Fine. But you understand this goes no further than the four of us, or I turn everyone in. Got it?"

"We've got it, Idris," Warren says.

"So, this thing you've found, have you seen any more of it?" Idris asks.

"No," I tell them, "but nobody else has come from Old Earth, and our supplies have been coming from Terra 5."

"Well, it's a nasty thing. It replicates faster than OEV, and nothing we have on the station is prepared to deal with whatever happens when it gets loose."

"Makes sense we don't let it loose then, right?" Kira suggests.

"You're so smart," Idris snaps, "you have any ideas about how to handle this?"

"Not yet. Do you?"

"Not yet."

"None of our medications will work against this virus?" I ask.

"Nothing so far. I haven't been able to get the fifth generation anti-virals yet, but I'm not hopeful. It's as if we're chasing a transport ship with spitballs."

26.

Jessie's lying in her bunk, watching a movie, when we come in. Kira has her boots off and is half way out of her suit when Jessie presses pause.

"C'mon, guys. Where were you that you stink so bad?"

"Sorry, Jess," I tell her. "It won't smell for long. Are you showering first, Kira?"

"Sure. Both bathrooms looked open, though." She takes her towel and shower kit with her.

"Seriously, Lacy, what did you step in, and why didn't you scrub down at the landing bays?"

"I didn't step in anything. You're just making up stuff." I put my boots and dirty suit by the door.

"You smell like a recycling center. Is that where you were?" Jessie suddenly sits up. "Is that where she gets all her electronics? I've never seen anyone have so many flash drives, and those memory chips,"

"We were playing ball on 13C. Some of the guys weren't wearing any shirts, okay?"

"13C is next to the recycling center."

"Maybe some of the air came through the vents. Do you have any neutralizing spray?"

"It'll cost you two credits."

"Forget it."

"Come on, Lacy. I can't take this smell in here all night."

"Let me use your spray then."

"One credit." I don't answer her. "Lacy, please. At least store them outside in the common area." Tempting, but no. Wait for her. "Fine. You're killing me. Don't expect me to be nice all the time, okay?" She gets her odor neutralizing spray from her closet and throws it at me. "Next time won't be free, and I won't be as accommodating."

"Thank you, Jessie." Spray our boots, spray our suits, get my towel and shower kit, and off to the other bathroom in our unit.

27.

My chief and two lieutenants are speaking with the station master in the chief's office. It's never good when the station master comes here this early. Maybe it's a third shift problem.

"Someone's getting fired," one of the J3s says.

"What're you talking about?" I ask.

"Why else would a station master be here?"

"How long have they been in there?"

"They were here before us," the J3 tells me. That's really not good.

The chief comes out of her office. "Harrison. Good. In here, please." The door hisses closed behind us. "We seem to have a problem here." Is the fat man making waves again? Maybe they know about the fungus. Although Warren has it now so that should be all his problem.

"We need another decon specialist for third shift," the station master explains, "and you've been chosen."

"I don't understand," comes from my mouth. I must be in trouble for something. Someone must've found out about Kira giving us more credits.

"Third shift needs an S1."

"I don't understand," I repeat. "Why am I being demoted?"

"You're not being demoted, you're just being switched to third shift," the chief explains. "When they find another decon specialist, you'll come back to first shift." That'll never happen because we're not taking any more people on. Maybe if one of the tweens grows up some, but that won't be for a while. Third shift. I've only worked third shift when someone got sick or we had an Earth Executive visit, and everyone was working doubles.

"It'll be better for your schooling, too, if you think about it," the chief continues. "Now you can stay with your classmates." I'm ahead of my "classmates" in every subject except math. "And, if you finish your school work early, you can be promoted early as well." Nobody from third shift has been promoted in my lifetime here. "So, in the interest of time, you'll clean out your locker, and you start your new shift tonight. Your lieutenant will check in any equipment or supplies that don't belong to you. Do you have any questions?"

"No, ma'am."

"Then we're finished here," the station master says. Great. The junior lieutenant gets his tablet and follows me to my locker.

Bio detector goes back, so does the extra box of respirator cartridges.

"You can keep the respirator," the lieutenant tells me. That's good because I don't want to spend another three days getting fitted for a new mask. "Those are your gloves?"

"They're the ones I always use," I say.

"Eh, go ahead and keep those, too. Not like we don't have enough for our people."

Both the respirator and the gloves go into the small outside pouch on my duffel bag. Two clean suits, socks, underwear, and deodorant go into the bag itself.

"I guess that's it," I sigh.

"No digi screens or computers?"

"No, sir. I always use the one at the docking station."

"Okay. That's it then." Close up the bag, head to the café for an early brunch.

28.

There's nobody else within five tables of where I'm sitting in the cafe, and Idris has to start mopping here. I don't really want to talk to anyone – I'm still mad about the transfer.

"Hey, little one," he says, scrubbing the floor behind me.

"Hey."

"Heard you're on third shift now." I'm sure under and around my chair are now spotless. And how does he know these things already? I didn't even tell Warren yet.

"Too bad for me, right?"

"You can learn a lot on third shift," he smiles. "That's when most of the dirty work gets done. But you know that."

"I guess I'll have to leave all that up to you guys for now."

"Don't be sad, Lacy. You'll still pick up some stuff while you're working. We just need to be more careful, that's all."

"Speaking of careful,"

"Speaking of that, you have an interesting way of repaying favors, young lady."

"Really?" I always thought I'd owe him forever.

"Really. In fact, it seems I'm in your debt now." That I don't believe. He smiles a little. "Don't be so surprised. Just keep up the good work."

"I'll do what I can. Thanks." He moves away from me towards the junior grades sitting on the other side of the room.

29.

Now I know why Jessie likes to shower after the kids go to school - the hot water is actually hot. If only I could get some sleep before the little ones come back.

Kira comes into our room. She's looking at her old computer screen.

"Hey. What're you doing home so early?" I ask.

"It's my day off," she answers. "Are we the only ones here?"

"Gary's in his quarters."

"Can I show you something?"

"It's not a new OEV video, is it? I don't need to see any of that 'til next year,"

"No. That's not it. You know how my boss doesn't like to use his earpiece when he's in his office?"

"Yeah. So?"

"Well, he hardly empties the trash on his computer, too. Watch this."

"You hacked a station master's computer?"

"Not really. Just look." Kira shows me her computer and presses PLAY. The video shows an outpost hall with a bunch of bodies floating around, an explosion, then nothing.

"What is that?" I ask her.

"Outpost 8."

"No way. It looks like some of your 20th century stuff. It must've been a high quality digitization,"

"I'm telling you it's a video feed from the station, Lacy."

"Okay, say it's Outpost 8. How would they get a bomb through security?"

"It didn't go through security. Look; it took out the whole station." She plays the clip again.

"C'mon, Kira, seriously. They're probably just offline or something."

"My station master checked. There's nothing there anymore."

"They were at capacity. We would've heard when they evacuated that many people."

"They didn't evacuate anyone, Lacy." She closes the file.

"They wouldn't kill 20,000 people, Kira. And where did you get that video? It still looks like a bad movie from Mars Colony."

"It's a feed from the outpost. All the station masters got it the other day." I should know better than to ask anything more. "I don't know who sent it; I couldn't get past the Old Earth firewalls without being traced."

"Are you sure someone from Old Earth sent this?"

"As far as I can see. Usually I can tell if someone's bouncing a signal off the satellites."

"You can't get caught, Kira."

"Don't worry about me, Lacy. We need to think about everyone here. They blew up the whole station."

After a minute I say, "Warren would know what to do."

"He's not far enough up the food chain to know anything."

"What about Idris?" I ask. "He knows about everything on this station."

"He's not senior grade, though, is he?"

"No, but that's just because they refuse to promote him. He's had so many jobs here, he's pretty much invisible."

"We need to be completely invisible if we're going to stay alive." She may be right about that.

30.

So much for sleep. Not even documentaries on how plants used to grow on Old Earth work as sedatives. 2200 comes too quickly.

"You really have to work third shift?" Kira asks.

"Yup. I don't need the overhead light."

"Oh, I don't care about that. Do what you need to do."

Socks, suit, boots on. Grab my toothbrush and washcloth, head to the bathroom. The rest of the kids are confined to their rooms.

"Hey." Gary sounds surprised.

"Hey. I'm still working third shift."

"That's right. I totally forgot. Are you going to be all right with that? Maybe we need to find you quieter quarters." I only lived with one other unit parent when I was little. I've been here with Gary for almost seven years now. "It's fine if you want to stay, Lacy, but maybe where more people work third shift?"

"I'll see how it goes," I tell him. "Anyway, I'm going to a singles dorm in a little while."

"That's true. Well, I hope it's quiet enough for you."

"Thanks." Into the bathroom I go.

If only I could stay awake tonight. Not even the industrial cleaner keeps my eyes open. I stand up to finish my section of Docking Bay 18C-24.

"What, you can't reach?" one of the J3s laughs.

"I can get the important places," I respond. "Looks as if you can't see well enough, though."

He looks around and sees the spots he missed. "At least I don't need a ladder," he grumbles.

My comm beeps. SEE YOU @ 0815. No sender, no time stamp. Some kid's probably playing with the computers again. Doesn't matter - I'll be on my way home by then. My comm beeps again.

"What is that, your boyfriend or something?" The J3 comes over, but I hide my screen from him.

"It's yours saying he wants you home right away."

"Whatever. You don't have to be stupid about things." He goes back to wiping down the taller half of the airlock. My comm reads DON'T LEAVE EARLY. Again without the identifying stamp. I erase both messages and go to work on the lower half of the airlock.

31.

I'm eating at a diner on 18B today, and Warren still finds me. I really need to sleep.

"Here you are," he says, looking at my food. "What are you doing all the way out here?"

"Dinner. Why?" Real eggs are SO much better than the junk we get in the cafes. The extra credits from Kira really do come in handy.

"Didn't you get a message?"

"I get a lot of messages." He sits across from me and takes a piece of my toast.

"You really should read them as you get them,"he says. "This is pretty good. Is this natural bread?"

"As far as I know. What do you want, Warren? I've been up for 27 hours."

"Straight? No wonder you're cranky. Are you going to eat those eggs?"

"Yes. Take the juice if you want something."

He eats more of the toast. "Well, the reason you got a message is we're about to have another problem."

"Why? The Earth man still trying to bill us for his leather bag?"

"Someone here has come down with an unknown virus." I almost choke on my food. "I know. We don't know for sure what it is, but it looks bad."

"I thought we had the only sample."

"Apparently not."

"The End-Life people?" They've been trying to end all human life for about a hundred years. If this is them, they've gotten a lot more coordinated and much bolder than before.

"No. I don't know," he says.

"We didn't do this, did we?"

"No way. We're too good."

"You're sure?" Three security officers come in and sit next to us. All S3s.

"Absolutely. Check in with your roommate," Warren mutters. He finishes my juice then stands.

"See you later?" I smile politely.

"Maybe. We have a lot of schoolwork to catch up on." He disappears into the crowd outside the diner. Great. Now I'm too wired to sleep.

32.

At least there isn't a waiting list to get into this learning lab. I can take my time with these ancient texts. Except now I'm getting crazy pop-ups on my screen. *Beowulf* isn't hard enough without these things. But I'm not going to be the one who unleashes a computer virus in a learning lab. 11 messages in the last 22 minutes. I ought to report this as harassment. If I knew where they're coming from. Before I can decide what to do, Kira slides into the space next to me.

"Don't you ever check your messages?" she whispers.

"Don't you know we're not supposed to open anything suspicious?"

"Anyway, Warren said he talked to you?"

"And? I have four more chapters to translate before I do anything else."

"What he said is true."

"I told him real eggs are much better than hash, especially for dinner."

"Nice, Lacy. We're going to die, and you're doing homework."

The security guard stands up and looks at us. "What're you two doing?"

"Sorry," I tell him. "We'll be quiet." I go back to *Beowulf,* and he sinks back into his seat.

"We have to do something," Kira hisses.

"Like?"

"I thought you might have an idea."

"Idris got an A in microbiology."

"You're in microbiology now. Well, anyway, this is viruses."

"I don't know. Although, ... No, I don't know."

"What, Lacy? Any idea is a good one now."

"All right. What time do you get out of work?"

"1600 I hope. I'll message the guys. Please check your messages?" She heads out of the lab.

"Sure." A little more than four hours to kill.

33.

I think this is the sixth or eighth time I've read this passage. There's nothing on the page for my translation. Haven't heard from Kira, so it is definitely time to go to bed. I don't remember all these people coming into the learning lab. I'll take the elevator in C sector instead of wading through the people on the 18th deck. My comm beeps. DON'T GO HOME. No sender, no time stamp. I don't care. I'm too tired to play games.

Get off the elevator, red and white emergency lights are flashing. Turn the corner there's a decon tent set up in the middle of the hall, lots of security hanging around. Some of the people have oxygen tanks and masks on. I bet Scott made a stink bomb again and let it loose in the hall. I don't know why they still let him into the science labs if he's going to keep playing around.

"Excuse me," I say to the security chief in the hallway. "What's going on? My unit's just down the hall," I stop when he snatches my ID and two large security officers grab my arms.

"Give me your right hand," the chief barks. One of my captors holds my right hand to a palm reader. "Don't bother fighting; it'll only make things worse." Then they cuff my hands behind my back.

"I don't understand. What is happening?"

"Don't play stupid, young lady. Take her to 18D. We'll settle this there."

18D has a holding center for judicial processing. I wish someone would tell me what's going on. The security officers don't let go even in the elevator.

"Can I know what I'm being charged with at least?" No answer. "I'm not going to run anywhere. I mean, where would I go? I don't have authorization to take a pod or shuttle or anything. And someone has my ID." Still nothing.

Scan my right hand before putting me into a black cell with black bars by myself. My hands are still tied behind me. A gray bench is bolted to the floor. The walls must be reinforced with something that makes the room so small. Two guys, even bigger than the security officers, stand guard over the holding cells.

"Hey," I say to one of them, "am I under arrest? If I am, I request an attorney. Do you hear me? I need my lawyer."

"You need to be quiet," he responds.

Two more sets of guards later, a security chief comes to my cell. I stand at attention as best I can.

"Lacy Harrison?"

"Yes, sir."

"Come with me." He slides the gate open, and we go to another room. Black floor, dark walls, dark panels even on the ceiling. Nothing there except two orange chairs and a small gray table. I know there's a camera somewhere, but I don't see it. The fat man from Old Earth comes in behind us. I wonder who knows he's still here. The security chief sits me away from the door.

"Hello, Specialist," the Earth man smiles.

"You two know each other?" the chief demands.

"We've met before," the visitor says.

"Am I under arrest?" I ask again.

"You're a person of interest," the chief responds. Did Kira get caught with her computer stuff? "What's your position on this outpost?"

"Senior Grade 1 Decontamination Specialist." Maybe they found Warren's hiding place with all his secret things.

"And you work on first shift?"

"No, sir. I was transferred to third shift two weeks ago."
He should know that already.

"You were scheduled to be sleeping at 1200 hours, weren't
you?"

"I thought I could get some translations done for school
after work."

"Why did you check out of your work shift early two nights
ago?"

"I took my ten minute break at the end of the shift because
I had to go to the bathroom. My supervisor said it was okay."
They should know that already, too.

The visitor leans close to me, breathing in my face. "During
your work, Specialist, if you found an illegal substance on the
station, you'd report it, wouldn't you?" It smells as if he's got garlic
breath, but it's a little more sour than that.

"Yes, sir," I answer.

"To whom would you report it?" the fat man continues.

"I would first speak with my direct supervisor, and then I'd
make sure a report was filed with the chief on duty." What is he
trying to do?

"In fact, you would report any anomaly during decontamination, wouldn't you?"

"Yes, sir."

"Like the false bottom in my tool box."

"Yes, sir."

"In fact, what did the scan show in that box?"

"It read as something organic but nothing we usually check for. Chief, sir, we quarantined the box, and my lieutenant took it from there."

"So you had no idea nerve agent was brought onto this station?" What is the chief talking about? Idris didn't say anything about nerve agent. The only thing I know about that is there's a stockpile on Old Earth in the desert somewhere. And you have to be a technician or above to move canisters or tubes of pretty much anything.

"It wasn't brought on during third shift," I tell them. "Not since I've been there."

"And what about first shift?"

"Not in 18C, Chief. We would've heard about it before now." Is that what they were doing on deck 3A?

The Earth man moves towards the door. "What is your experience with nerve agent or any other noxious gas?"

"None, sir. Not even in Chem lab. I mean, I read about them for class, but handling them? Never."

"Never. Not even stink bombs."

"Personally? I've been a victim of a stink bomb or two, but I don't know anything about making them." What happened to my unit?

The men are quiet for a minute. The chief asks, "Where were you at 1200 hours?"

"I was in a learning lab, 16D. Could you please tell me what's going on?"

"You're saying you really don't know?"

"That's what I'm saying, sir."

"Fine. Be that way." The chief knocks at the door. Two security techs step in, and the other men step out.

34.

At least they've taken the cuffs off my hands. I must've slept because I don't remember this guard coming on duty. I wonder how Security gets their guys so huge. Maybe if all I drank were protein shakes, I too could grow up big and strong.

"Hello?" I try. "Excuse me, I need to pee." Nothing from the man. I guess I'll have to go in the corner if they don't let me out of here soon.

"I don't understand it either, sir, but the forms are in order." That sounds like Warren.

A pause. "She's in 25A," someone else says. "Show these to the next guy."

Sure enough, it's Warren with his computer. "Good morning, sir. I'm here to take custody of the prisoner."

"Says who? I didn't get those orders."

"Well, here we go." The guard looks at the computer. Scroll up, scroll down. Scrutinize every signature on the form. Satisfied with his findings, the guard holds his ID to the scanner, and the gate to my cell opens.

"She can get her belongings at the clerk's desk."

"Thanks," Warren says.

Twenty minutes later, my stuff is in my pockets, I've stopped at a restroom, and we are on our way, I hope, to 14C.

"Do you have any idea how much trouble you're in?" he asks me quietly. "Kira had to get around two firewalls to get you released."

"I don't even know what's going on, Warren. Why were they decontaminating my hall? Where's Gary? He should've been notified by now that I was in trouble." We stop walking.

"You seriously don't know?"

"Know what? Warren, c'mon."

"Someone gassed your unit. The ones on all sides got affected, too, but they didn't die."

"What? Wait. People died?" I don't understand.

"Everyone who was in the unit is gone."

"Gary? Jessie? Blainey?"

"Kira was in the command center, but everyone else is no more. Finished."

"Even the little ones?"

"Even the kids, Lacy. They really didn't tell you anything?"

"Just that I was a person of interest. How did that stuff get onto the station, Warren? What is happening?"

"I don't know. Nobody does. Let's get you settled in a singles dorm, and then you can eat. Kira's already in a place on 17B." A singles dorm sounds crowded, but food sounds good.

35.

17B unit 224. There're only thirteen of us in this unit – it should be quieter than with the kids around.

"There's two senior lieutenants in the first room," Warren says, still looking at his computer. "They're in charge of the unit. You're here in the third room."

"Next to the bathrooms." Where the water is running.

"Better than an elevator. I know you're a senior grade, but we're still short rooms. Housing will figure something out soon." His computer beeps. "Okay. You're all set. You've officially been released from custody." He touches his screen. "I sent you a copy of all your forms, including the arrest warrant. You should be okay to go back to work tonight."

"Great. Thank you, Warren."

"I didn't do anything. You need to thank Kira for all the maneuvering. I have to go back to work, but talk to Kira or Idris. They may know what's going on."

"Sure. Do you want to meet later?" I ask him.

"I'll see what I can do. You should get some rest."

"Yeah, okay. Have fun at work then." Warren heads out, and I go into my room.

My stuff is on the lower left bunk. Everything still smells like disinfectant spray. Open the first closet, there's someone's junior suits hanging there. More in the second closet. I'll chat with that person later about sharing. In the meantime, there are some empty drawers under my bunk.

"Hey." Kira stands in the doorway. "I thought I heard you guys."

"Hey. I didn't know you were here." I definitely need some closet space for my suits. And where's my lock box?

"Surprise. My boss gave all the trainees an extra day off this week -- something about getting caught up with our school work. Did everything go okay?"

"Yeah. Thanks for springing me." What would anyone want with my things?

"No problem," Kira says. "They tried to take your extra credits, too, but I got them stored in a safe place. Oh, and this is yours." She holds out my box.

"Thanks." All my pictures are still here, as is my watch.

"Does it still work?" I shake the watch a little. It starts ticking.

"Looks that way." I slip the watch into my pocket. "Is Jessie really dead?"

"Apparently. Gary, too. It's a little crazy." She checks her computer. "Did they tell you what happened?"

"Warren did. The guy from Old Earth asked some questions, too."

"He's still here?" Kira's a little surprised. "I doubt he said anything about bringing the virus here."

"I think he was trying to find out who has it. Any word on another station-wide decon?"

"The sick person is just visiting from outpost 12. He's in quarantine 'til they can figure out what to do."

"Fabulous. What else can go wrong?"

"Well, someone from Old Earth has been messaging the second shift station master a lot lately. Most of them are stuff for some exploration company."

"Not our visitor?"

"No. It's coming from outside our star system."

"The station master could be an investor."

"They're too big to be just stock reports. I bet there's embedded files there, too. I saved a couple to my drive, but I haven't had time to look at them."

"Do you really think he's involved?"

"How else does all this stuff get onto the station?"

"Should I ask how you get the second shift station master's mail?"

"The same way I get the other files. You don't have to worry, Lacy. I'm extra careful with that stuff."

"Good. I'd hate to see you deported for stupid things."

"Thanks. Y'know, not for nothing, I'm glad you were studying the other day."

"I'm glad you were working," I tell her.

"Well, I'm off to the learning lab. See you later?"

"Sure. Message me." Kira heads out, and I go back to putting my things away.

36.

They really did take away my money. I hardly have enough to get a decent meal at the cafe.

"Hey, kid, make a decision already."

"Two sandwiches, please." The hash looks particularly gross tonight. Grab a drink, swipe my ID, listen to the beep telling me I have fewer than 10 credits on my account. The last time I had fewer than 10 credits, I was 12. And we don't get paid for another two days. There's an empty table in the far corner. It's not empty for long – Idris plants himself and his food right there. I sit with him anyway.

"What's new, little one?"

"Not much." Except he has real meat in his sandwiches.

"Thought you'd be hungry," he says.

"How many favors would I owe you?"

"None. C'mon. I know they didn't feed you on the 18th deck."

"Does this constitute you paying me back?" I'd rather have him owing me a favor than him feeding me badly made food.

"Call it a business lunch. No favors changed hands." I take a sandwich and some potatoes from his plate. "Your roommate get you up to speed?" he asks.

"Sure."

"She said you had an idea as to how to fix the problem."

"I don't know anything about the gas attack."

"You haven't aggravated someone lately?"

"Nobody since the Earth man," I say.

"You sure?"

"Maybe some J3s on third shift, but I don't think they're smart enough to pull this off."

"Careful about J3s," he reminds me. "They can surprise you."

"I know, but they're not like you or Jessie." I'm really going to miss her.

"What about the other problem?" He passes me more potatoes.

"What about it?"

"Any idea can be a good one."

"I don't think it'll work."

"We could still try, though, right?"

"Okay," I say. "So I thought the fungus or whatever that was from 3A could do something to the new virus. But the scientists should've thought of that already."

"Maybe it doesn't work." He wolfs down his last sandwich.

"Maybe there isn't enough stuff to go around."

"Let's see what happens. Here. Take some more food."

"No, I'm good. Thanks." We finish eating in relative silence.

37.

The loading docks at 18C are particularly quiet tonight. No ships have stopped here in three weeks, so there's really nothing to do. A few J3s are working on the airlock, I have the computers and office area to clean. I hope they don't make us clean the escape pods next. Some people like to shoot the pods off by "accident," and they're a real pain to reattach to their airlocks. I guess the pods aren't meant to come back once they've left.

"Shutup, stupid," one of the J3s says quietly.

"Go ask her if you want to," another one whispers.

"You ask her. I'm not the one who cares."

"Ask me what?" I stand in the office doorway.

"Nothing," the first one smiles.

"Who's got the bet going?" I ask. Their red faces tell me they're not in charge of the gambling. "C'mon. You might as well tell me. I am your boss."

"Promise you won't get mad," the first one says.

"You're stalling."

"Well," the second one starts, "there's whether or not you were charged, and then there's how long you were going to be in custody, and then there's whether or not you'd be demoted,"

"And there's whether they'd keep you in decon or not," the first one finishes.

"I wasn't charged with anything," I state loud enough for everyone to hear, "I was in custody for 20 hours, and there's no reason for me to be demoted or transferred, so, clearly, you're still stuck with me. That about cover it?"

"Sure, boss. Thanks," someone else says. Maybe I'll get one of them to clean the pods.

38.

Cafe 14B is no different than 14C. Too bad. Too bad it's two credits for a full meal. Kira said she'd get me some of my extra credits back when she could. Gary used to talk about full meals coming from real animals and plants before OEV and before the deserts formed.

"Hey." I jump at the sight of Warren sitting at my table. "Sorry," he says. "What're you thinking about so intently?"

"I thought the food would be better here."

"You're kidding, right? C'mon, Lacy. What's up?"

"Nothing. I'm tired." Idris comes out from the printing area, a bag in hand. "What is this, a party?" I ask.

"We're going to test your theory," Warren whispers.

"Morning, Little Lacy." Idris puts the bag on my tray. "Have some."

"Another working lunch?"

"They came from above," Idris says. "Warren, you, too." Warren takes out a sticky bun. I haven't seen one of these in I don't know how long.

"Where did you find this?" Warren finishes it in three bites. "You'd better have one, Lacy. I could eat all these right now." Idris and I take the three remaining buns out of the bag. Yeah, this is better than I remembered. "It's good, right? Idris, man, you're the best."

"So what brings us together?" I suck the syrup off my fingers.

"I'm on recycling duty," Idris starts. This is not news. "I thought we could experiment with our visitor in quarantine."

"Wouldn't it be better if I do it?" I ask. Whatever "it" is. "I mean, it's probably easier for decon to get into his room than recycling."

"Someone's got to get the trash, right? Anyway, I'm under the radar for now."

"I think it's safe to say we're all being watched," Warren says quietly.

"Yes, but I'm supposed to be places nobody else goes," Idris responds.

"Kira can get me assigned to the medical zone," I offer.

"Please just let me do this." Warren waits a moment then puts his hand into the bag.

"Darn. There aren't any more sticky buns."

"We good?" Idris asks. He crumples up the bag and puts it in his pocket.

"It's all there," Warren mutters.

"We're good," I add. Idris smiles a little then disappears into the printing area. Warren takes half of the last bun.

"I'll beep you later," he says then heads out of the café. I wolf down the rest of my dinner so I can enjoy the last of our treat.

39.

It's quiet in my room – just two of us here, one of us sleeping. I don't know why I'm awake all of a sudden. Nobody's using the bathroom near my bunk. My comm says 1300. I've only slept two hours. Check my comm again, there's another anonymous message – a link to a site I've never heard of. I put my headphones on just in case there's sound.

Old black and white video of stuff burning - I can't make out what it is under the flames and smoke. The screen goes white then black then gray again as a mushroom cloud appears on the screen. Something through night vision glasses, green and black people running for their lives, a lighter green mist being sprayed over them. I turn the video off before it can make me sick. A pop-up appears - "Don't let this continue. You know what to do." Then it and the video delete themselves. Who sent this to me? Kira's working. So is Warren. Maybe Idris found something. Although Kira's the only one I know slick enough to delete the files. Three hours 'til someone gets off duty. I won't panic. I'll try to rest a little 'til we can sort things out.

40.

Someone said a hot shower was as good as a rest. Someone should've told engineering that 25°C isn't even warm. Maybe I can catch a game on deck 13. I haven't been swimming in a long time either. Maybe they have a hot shower. Except my comm beeps. It's Idris. COME TO 14D RECYCLER 23 @ 1630. USE C SECTOR ELEVATOR. Great - another smelly evening.

Warren's already in the "capture" center with Idris. This is a dangerous place because it's where they collect the radioactive elements and the particles that won't recycle into something new. There is a lot of equipment on the clear counter top. Two gray forensics boxes are next to what looks like a centrifuge.

"Don't we need suits?" I ask.

"No," Idris says, turning away from the monitor, "this is the clean room." If by clean he includes the stink of garbage and the possibility of a nuclear accident. This is where they do quality control," Idris says, "they check samples to see how well the collectors work. "Kira's not with you?" A beep at the door. We look at the monitor - there she is. Idris locks the door behind her.

"Nice place, guys," Kira says. "I'm supposed to be in a learning lab at 1930 hours."

"You should probably go then," Warren suggests. "We don't know how long this will take."

"No, I'm staying," Kira tells him. "We're all in this together, right?"

"So we're here to figure out how to use this stuff." Idris pulls out a large vial of fungus. Brown with black and white streaks through it, and it almost fills the container.

I'm trying not to sound stupid, but I ask anyway, "How'd you grow so much of it?"

"It seems that it likes fresh food as much as we do," Idris says. "There's about half the sample you gave me, Lacy, that I left alone, but I just wanted to see what would happen if it was exposed to different things."

"What did you find out?" Warren beats me to the same question.

"Well, as I said, it grew best in fresh stuff, like the meat or the protein in the hash from the cafes. The only thing that can hold it is glass."

"Have you diluted it yet?" I ask.

"Not with fluids. You want to try?"

We all put gloves on, and Idris and I unpack the first forensics box. Empty glass tubes; containers with water, alcohol, transparent blue stuff, and a couple other clear liquids; a bag of blood, close enough to its expiration date that it should be recycled; biohazard bags.

"Can't we use their equipment?" Warren asks. The second forensics box has a variety of slides, more empty glass tubes, and a bunch of empty, different-sized glass vials. There's even a microscope in the box.

"I wouldn't," I say. "Just in case we mess up. And we don't want to cross-contaminate anything."

Kira takes the plug and puts it into the nearest outlet. "Will they be tracking the power use?" she wonders out loud.

"This unit's down for repair 'til next week," Idris tells us. "All the readings from here are a little off."

Out comes the vacutainer with the fat man's virus in it. That goes on the other side of the counter from us.

"Maybe only one of us should be touching this," Idris suggests. "So nobody makes a mistake?"

"We've all had science lab," Warren says.

"Idris is the only one with real skills, though," Kira points out.

"So I'll do the mixing then," he pronounces. I wish I had my face mask on – just in case.

Idris lays out some slides. They're thicker than most - they have a well in the center, where you'd be looking under the microscope. Then come the syringes and droppers. I still feel under-dressed without our safety gear. Maybe there's a suit in the closet here that'll fit me.

Reading my mind, Warren says, "Relax, Lacy. We wouldn't be here if it wasn't safe." I hope he's right.

Cut a sliver of the fungus, store that in a tube. Ten drops of a clear liquid, close up the tube with a glass stopper. Shake it up 'til the fluid is grayish brown. This isn't going to work.

"Put some blood on a slide," Idris says. Three big drops go into the well of a slide. He puts two drops of his concoction onto the same slide then puts the slide onto the microscope.

"Anything?" Kira asks.

"Nothing good," Idris responds. "We've got a long way to go." Four hours and twenty mixtures later, "This is it!"

"Are you sure?" Warren asks.

"Here. Touch your glove to the solution," Idris tells him.

Warren pulls back. "I don't want any of that crap eating my hand, thanks. You touch it." I put my finger onto the slide. No ill effects.

"That's pretty cool," Kira admits. "And it's working on the virus?"

"See for yourself," Idris says. "If there's any left." Sure enough, there are only pieces of the green virus cells on the slide.

"Won't this stuff feed on the blood cells, too?" I ask.

"It doesn't seem to. Here." Idris puts a drop of blood onto the slide, then a drop of the virus. Sure enough, the green cells are broken apart by the tan stuff, and most of the red cells are left alone. I wonder if it'd work on OEV. I wonder if we'd get credit for figuring out the cure for this mess.

"We should replicate our findings before we get excited." Count on Warren to make sense. "I mean, I don't want to kill the mood, but we only have one shot at this."

"How much virus do we have left?" Kira asks.

Idris checks the green fluid. "We're good for a few more tries."

"What about the fungus?"

"I have two more whole vials."

"Let's go then," Warren proclaims. Idris lines up all the supplies and starts the experiment again.

41.

2300 hours. Time to get up and go to work. The girl in the bunk above me is still watching movies on her digi screen.

"Did I wake you up?" she asks.

"No, I'm on third shift."

"Crap. I'm sorry. See you in the morning then."

I smile politely, get my suit on, and head for the bathroom. Kira's in the common area, glued to her digi screen. She takes her headphones off when she sees me.

"Do you know what time it is?" I ask her.

"Actually, I do, thanks. I found a couple old Mars Colony movies I've never seen before."

"And you're going to watch that crap this late at night?"

"Well, one of the lieutenants goes to the gym at 0400, and two of my roommates are on third shift, so I won't be alone for long. What about you? Did you get any sleep?"

"Some. It was good we finished quickly."

"Let's see what happens before we get excited."

"No kidding. See you later."

"G'nite." She goes back to her movie, I go into the bathroom.

42.

"Prepare docking station for arrival," the computer states. This is highly irregular. Hardly any ships come in at 0300, unless it's supposed to be a secret.

"Suit up, boss," a J2 smiles. "We're actually going to work for our credits tonight."

"Wanna bet who's on it?" a J3 suggests. I grab the suit that fits me best and wait by the decon area. It's quieter here than where the ship actually lands. Who's trying to keep something under the radar? Is the guy from Old Earth bringing more stuff here? I wonder if the station master knows about this. I know I'll get in trouble for not going up the chain of command if I report something, especially if this turns out to be nothing.

"Docking is imminent," from the computer. That means the guys have ten minutes to put their suits on and hook onto the tethers that keep them from floating away when the bay depressurizes. Some people think they're funny and tie a knot in the tethers, but that only kinks the air tubes and makes it hard to breathe in those suits.

The shuttle from Terra 5 lands perfectly. "Bay doors secured, re-pressurization complete." The real surprise is there's only two pallets of food printer elements and three pilots onboard. Why do they need to send a shuttle with almost no supplies? Our lieutenant verifies the cargo, and two guys shift the boxes into the decon area. Now it's my turn.

The section chief, another lieutenant, and the man from Old Earth appear from around the corner. The visitor is carrying his own bags. He says something to the section chief; neither is too happy. One of the pilots helps the Earth man through the airlock, and they are on their way somewhere.

"What's the problem, Harrison?" The section chief's voice booms through my suit.

"No problem, sir." Just wondering why the fat man had to leave at this hour, why didn't the pilots stay their required six hours rest time, am I going to have any more trouble now that the visitor has left.

"Can Sustenance take their crates yet?"

"Yes, sir. All clear." I would've thought people would be less grouchy with one fewer person onboard. 0600. Shower, write my report, hope nothing else comes up in the next two hours.

43.

"Everyone will get a look at the slides," the lab instructor tells us. It's too early for me to be awake, but I don't want to ruin my perfect attendance for this class. "Record your thoughts and observations on your computers. I'd like to see if anyone has a good idea for what's happening."

Wait a few minutes then look into the first microscope. Crap - it's a blood sample with the new virus mixed in. Green cells destroying the red ones, then splitting into two more green ones. I wonder who this came from. Maybe the man who brought it here in the first place? Maybe there's more than one person infected on this station? On to the next table.

"You don't want to look some more?" the kid behind me asks. Must be a really smart trainee to get into this class.

"No, I'm good," I say. "Thanks."

"You must have an awesome memory then."

I smile politely then look in the second microscope. Red cells look normal, off-white ones are larger and slowly moving around the slide. A couple green cells, still and off to the side.

This has to be from the guy in quarantine. What do I say? I should probably play really dumb for this assignment.

"Are these samples from the same source?" the trainee asks.

"Yes," our teacher answers.

"How much time elapsed between the two samples?" from someone else.

"72 hours."

"Is there a specific antidote we're looking for?"

"Write it down," the instructor tells the trainee.

What to write. How did this happen? What are those beige cells? How did the green ones die off? How did our lab instructor get these samples? I guess it's good Idris gave the patient the fungus. I can honestly say I don't know what this is about.

44.

Kira is sitting at the farthest table in cafe 14B, playing with her old computer. Idris is standing over her.

"What do you want, kid?" The food server isn't wearing her gloves.

"Is that mac and cheese?" Not that it smells all that different than the protein hash. At least Kira gave me back some of my extra credits, so now I have a choice.

"It's two credits for a serving."

"I'll take it. Thanks." Grab a drink, swipe my ID, go sit with Kira and Idris.

"Are you sure this is going to work?" he asks.

"Pretty sure," Kira answers. "This is the account all the official messages come from to my boss."

"The word is out?" I ask.

"About the cure? Not exactly. They just know the guy from Outpost 12 is getting better."

"I thought you were going to alert the media," I say.

"Oh, I will," she answers, "but I wanted the executives to get the message first. I'm tracking its progress now."

"You can do that with this computer?" Idris almost laughs.

"Don't let the case fool you. I have a 2 tera solid state and a 4 gig processor in here."

"Should we ask how that happened?" Idris asks.

"Nope."

"How long will it take to for the message to get to Central Control?" is my question.

"A couple hours tops from when it was sent. I flagged it as 'essential,' so it should be sent along pretty quickly."

"We're going to need to lose that computer," Idris tells Kira.

"I don't think so. I sent the main message from the command center." I won't ask how. "We should hear back soon."

"What if it's intercepted?" I ask. I can't be the only one worrying about this.

"Then I guess we're all done for," Kira answers.

45.

Now I remember why people come to the end of the deck.
I might as well be alone here, and I get a clear view of the
universe. Well, part of the universe. Deck 18 gives the best view –
90 degrees of nothing but stars. If you look carefully from Deck
18, you might see the sparkling light from Outpost 15. Terra 5 is
off to the left and down 30 degrees, about 12 hours away by
shuttle. Terra 4 is to the right, about 16 hours away. I wonder
where our help is coming from, if they're coming at all. I hope Idris
has an idea of how we can stay alive on this tin can.

46.

Music From the 2100s can get pretty loud at times. Maybe I'll switch to the 1800s to sleep to. Pounding on the outside door. Someone else can get it.

"All residents front and center!" Four security guards and a lieutenant - all J2s and J3s - are already searching the first room when I get to our common area. Kira doesn't look nearly as nervous as her three roommates.

"I want to know where that signal is coming from!" the lieutenant barks. One of the guards brings out a lighter and two magazines. Lighters have been banned since someone blew up the first terrapost trying to smoke a cigar indoors. I don't know what the problem is with the magazines. Maybe it's somebody's idea of porn or something immoral.

"Who's in charge of this unit?" the lieutenant demands.

"They're at work now," Kira volunteers. Two of the guards go into her room next. Kira still doesn't look nervous. I, however, am anxious on her behalf.

"Do you want to say something?" The lieutenant gets in the shortest girl's face. It's all she can do not to cry. They come out of Kira's room with her old laptop.

"Lieutenant." He scans the computer and is very upset with the results.

The officer looks squarely at Kira. "You're an IT trainee. What do you know about this renegade signal?"

"I'm sure I don't know what you're talking about, sir."

"How did you get to be an S2 already?"

"I guess my supervisor thought I was qualified, sir."

"And this relic?"

"A hand-me-down from my great-grandfather, sir. It only uses an ethernet port to communicate." The lieutenant scans the old computer then each of us individually.

"Sir, I don't think the signal is coming from here," one of the guards dares to say.

"Take that thing with us." And they all leave.

"Kira, where are all your flash drives and stuff?" a roommate asks. Kira takes her drives and chips from her pocket.

"You can relax," she tells us. "If I were stupid enough to send an unauthorized signal, it wouldn't originate from my quarters." The short girl lets some tears down her face. "It's okay, kid. They're just mad they can't find what they're looking for."

"I'm sorry they took your computer," I say.

"Don't be. It was something I won in a bet on Old Earth. My relic is here in my bag." Remind me to never get on Kira's bad side.

47.

An orange blinking border around my screen tells me I only have ten more minutes on the learning lab's computer. I definitely need more time with the endocrine system. Maybe there's room in the lab next door. A message from Idris – SEE YOU @ 1800. CAFÉ 14B. That's twenty minutes from now. Oh well – school work will have to wait.

Two meals in a row where I don't have to eat protein hash. Am I glad Kira got some of my credits back. Real string beans and a steak sandwich. I know the meat comes out of a printer, but they say it really tastes like a cow. I wonder what Terra 4 does with the animals in their zoo when they die. Before my mind wanders any further, Idris comes from the printing area. He has a tray of food with him.

"Someone got some extra credits," he smiles. "Still, you want some of this?"

"No, I'm good," I tell him. He eats a little before speaking.

"Help is definitely on the way," Idris says quietly.

"Who?"

"Terra 4, I think Kira said. She got the message a little while ago. Are you sure you don't want any applesauce?"

If I'd wanted something mushy for dinner, I would've had the hash. Instead, I ask, "What're we supposed to do?"

Warren appears at the near doorway. Seeing us, he heads right over.

"I don't know," Idris almost whispers. "What time do you have a break?"

"Hey, Warren. Sit with us?" I offer him part of my sandwich.

"No, we can't," he whispers. "You need to come with me now."

"Let me finish eating at least,"

"No, now." Warren yanks me out of my seat and cuffs my hands behind my back. He continues softly, "Idris, if you know what's good for you, you'll come, too."

"I don't know what you're pulling," Idris stops when we see four senior security officers come into the cafe. They're not interested in eating.

"C'mon," Warren says. "Both of you." Idris follows close behind.

"ID," demands the most senior security officer at the door. Warren shows his badge.

"I'm taking the prisoners back to the judicial center," Warren smiles.

"By yourself?" The senior officer isn't quite convinced.

"They're not interested in fighting," Warren says.

"Still. Someone should accompany you."

"We'll be fine, sir. You keep looking for the others." The security officer lets us go.

"Okay, you can take these things off me now." I turn so Warren can take the cuffs off, but he keeps hold of my hands.

"C'mon, Junior Patrolman," Idris mutters. "What's going on?" Warren shows a security bulletin on his comm. It has pictures of me and Idris wanted for robbery and assault.

"If you guys have any good ideas about how to get out of here," Warren says, "now's the time."

"Maybe if we don't walk down the main hallway here?" I suggest.

"If they're not tracking you now, they will be soon," Warren tells us."

"But we don't need to go to deck 18, do we?" Idris asks. Before Warren can answer, Kira barrels around the corner and stops just before she runs into us.

"Oh, good, we got to you first," she breathes.

"Not really," Warren says to her. "They've already alerted all of security."

Kira's computer beeps. "Crap," she lets slip. She starts typing at her computer.

"What is it?" I ask.

"They figured out I sent the message about the virus."

"Come with us then," Warren commands. "But first get rid of that thing."

"Gimme a second." Kira breaks the computer open, takes a couple chips and a hard drive, then drops the carcass into a recycle chute. "That should stop them for a minute or two," she says.

"What are you going to do without your computer?" I ask.

"Oh, don't worry," she almost laughs. "I've got two more here in my bag."

Four clangs of the bell, and the emergency lights start flashing. More bells ringing, and our comms beep. Warren looks at his comm – Kira has been added to the list of people wanted by security.

"That settles it," Warren sighs. "Promise you won't fight or run from me?"

"You're the best chance we have of surviving this mess, Officer," Idris says.

"Do you have any idea of how to get out of here?" Kira asks.

"No, but let's head towards 18D," Warren says.

Three young security patrolmen stand in the middle of the hall by the sector break. The red and white flashing lights are giving me a headache.

"Just keep walking," Warren mutters. "You're in my custody." The three security officers block our way.

"ID, please."

"What for?" Warren demands. "These people are witnesses to a crime."

"What crime?" The J2 reaches for Warren's ID badge. Warren snatches the boy's hand and twists it. "Hey!"

"Hey nothing, child. You are interfering with an investigation you are not a part of."

"You have just assaulted a senior officer," the J2 says.

"I doubt it," Kira says. "Look at his uniform; he's got three years on you." The J2 takes his hand back.

"You need to be quiet, trainee, if you know what's good for you."

Before I know it, Idris and Kira grab two guns and knock the disarmed security officers to the ground. Warren has his gun pointed at the third boy, a J3, who is aiming his weapon straight at me. I can see the young one is nervous – he can't hold his gun steady in one place.

"It's three against one," Idris points out.

"I can still take the two girls."

"Maybe one," Warren admits. "What's it going to be? Don't think we'd spare your friends here if you do something stupid."

"He probably doesn't even know how to use the thing," Idris smiles.

"Want to find out?" The boy's face is getting red, and now he's using two hands on the gun.

"Give it to me, and you live," Kira demands.

"Patrol never gives up their weapon."

"Patrol doesn't include being stupid," Idris says. "Give up the gun so you can live 'til tomorrow." The young man is clearly thinking things over.

"Don't do it," the J2 hisses.

"I don't care what you do," Idris responds. "Just make up your mind already."

"Okay. Okay." He slowly hands his weapon to Kira.

"Get up, you two," Idris says. They do. "Cuff them all together," Idris tells Kira. She puts the guns in her pockets, takes the security officers' handcuffs, and binds the three of them in a circle. "Take their badges, comms, and insignias." She does.

"Down the hall," Warren snaps. We waddle through the sector break and down the hall to a housekeeping closet. Kira opens the door with one of the guys' badges. There's not much room left. "Inside." The group falters. Idris points his gun at the J2's head.

"You wouldn't," the J2 snarls. Idris touches the weapon to the J2's temple.

"Be cool, man," one of the J3s says. "C'mon." They shuffle into the closet. Idris closes and locks the door behind them. Warren unlocks my hands and puts his cuffs away. Kira gives me a gun. Not that I have a clue how to use this. Warren reaches over and takes the safety off my weapon.

"Do you know how to use it?" Kira asks.

"Not really."

"Just aim and shoot," Idris says. "But be careful, the pulses trash everything, including the glass." Fabulous.

"We don't have much time," Warren says. "Someone's going to miss them soon."

48.

The doors to Sector D are closed. For now. The emergency lights are still flashing. At least the alarms have stopped sounding.

"What do we do?" I wonder.

"We need a strategy," Kira pronounces.

"I don't like this," Idris frowns. "We need to go the other way."

"Kira, can you jam all the sector breaks?" Warren asks. Ten seconds feels like a hundred years. Kira's computer finally beeps.

"Done."

"Stop right there!" Behind us are two older security officers, huffing and puffing, their guns drawn. Idris fires a warning shot over their heads, bringing down some ceiling tiles and a few loose wires. The lights down the hall go out. The officers freeze long enough for us to duck into a storage room.

"Hurry up and jam the lock," Idris yells. Kira types furiously. Warren shoots the door controls. "That'll do."

"Kira, can you get a floor plan for us?" Warren asks.

"Gimme a second."

So close, yet so far. The station schematics say there's another door here, but there isn't. Or at least, we haven't found it. We can hear the stomping of the security officers' boots outside our storage area. I hope they're not tracking our breathing.

"We should split up," Warren suggests almost silently.

"Four can watch all sides," Idris says. "Lacy, you have the inside, Kira, the outside. Warren, you've got our back." Scratching at the door. We can hear someone's ID being denied access to this area. They're talking out in the hall.

"Can we make a door?" Kira asks.

"Not without making a lot of noise," Idris responds. This means we're stuck.

"If we can get to level 18, we can spacewalk," I offer.

"They'll just collect us with a shuttle or something," Kira says.

"Not if they want us dead," Warren says. "Think about it. If we escape, we run out of air, they no longer have a problem, right?"

"Kira, can you program us a trip to Terra 4? That's the closest judicial center," Idris asks.

"Let's see what happens." Kira starts typing. The talking outside the holding area has stopped. Two more dings refusing the team access to our hiding area. "Crap." Now what? "There's a new class 1 firewall on the main server now."

"And that means?" Idris asks.

"I need a little time."

"How much is a little?" Boots are heading away from us.

"I'll let you know when I'm close."

"Wait," Warren says, "I've got it. We need to get to a closet or an access panel."

"We're going to hide in the closet 'til we get rescued?" Idris mopes.

"No. The reason they can't find my stuff is I hide it between the floors. I take the back panel off the closet and store my things in the space between floors."

"How does that get us to deck 18?" Kira asks.

"There's space between the walls, too. Maybe we can go up that way." I don't think this is a good idea.

Reading my mind, Idris sighs, "It's the only idea we have, right?" All we have to do now is find an access panel.

The things you don't know. I never thought Idris could fit in such a tiny space. I never knew there was enough room between the walls for grown people to slip through. The multicolored wires and red and white hoses are clipped together at the top of each deck. The vents are held in place with metal hooks. The ducts and walls are gray like the loading docks. Fortunately, there are little glow lights at each floor that are bright enough for us to see our way around. Idris stops above me.

"What's the matter?" Warren whispers.

"We've got a break ahead," Idris reports. "The wall above us is solid."

"What floor are we on?" Kira asks.

"16, I think," is my response.

"We're between 17 and 18," Idris says, "but I don't know where this opens up."

"We just have to get to the escape pods," Kira tells us. "It doesn't matter which one."

"So we need to be at 18A or C."

"They'll have a lot of security at the mechanicals in E sector," I point out.

"We're not that far over. Warren, do you have your plasma gun?"

"Here." He passes the weapon to me, and I pass it to Idris.

Idris moves to the left then to the right. I'm not sure how much longer these vent hooks are going to hold us. He comes back to where we are. "I'm pretty sure we're still in C sector. I don't see any security close by, but that doesn't mean anything. Ready to run?"

"Ready," we respond.

Idris raises the hatch and quickly sticks his gun out the opening. "We're in the middle of the sector," he whispers back to us before climbing onto the deck. The three of us get out just as easily. Red and white lights are still strobing in the hallway. I've got the inside, Kira the outside, Warren the back of our little group. Everybody has their guns ready to fire. We are in Sector C, so all we have to do is get to the loading docks and release the escape pod.

"What's the softest target?" Kira asks.

"Closer to Sector B," I respond. Oh, good, there's only two guards at that end of the hall.

"Let's go," Idris says. We stay as close to each other as possible.

"HEY! STOP RIGHT THERE!" The two security officers have their guns drawn. Idris fires once, hitting both guards. I look back to see Warren firing at guards from I don't know where. Kira shoots as well. She and Warren take care of the pursuit team. We keep running.

"HERE!" Escape Hatch 18C101. This gets us past the loading dock and directly onto the escape pods. Somebody's comm beeps – an alert telling security where we are. Open the hatch, there's two security guards there as well. Idris fires, one guard goes down. The other guard fires back. Warren goes down. Kira and Idris take out the rest of the guards who appear behind us while I check Warren. He's dead, too.

"C'mon, Lacy," Kira says. I can't move. I don't even care anymore. "Lacy, let's go. We need to get out of here, or it was all for nothing."

I empty his pockets, take his comm and badge. Then we close the hatch door, and Idris shoots the control panel to jam it shut. We hop into the fourth escape pod.

"You do not have authorization to disengage," the computer tells us. Kira starts typing at the control panel.

"Kira, get us out of here," Idris yells.

"Really? What did you think I was doing? Come on, come on." The pod lurches forward into the outpost wall then backwards towards space.

"You do not have BEEP BEEP BEEP Authorization complete," says the computer. Idris moves Kira away from the controls and flies this thing as fast as it will go.

49.

After what seems like a long time, "Are you sure we're not being followed?" Idris asks. He and Kira search the computers. I'm staring out the side window. Warren didn't need to die. None of this had to happen. I think I ought to be crying now, but I can't. We did all this for nothing. Maybe not nothing. Maybe there's a cure after all for these diseases. Maybe we started something for the scientists to work on.

"Nobody's behind us, but the monitor's picking up something big in front," Kira says. "Looks like a bunch of ships."

"I see them," Idris confirms. "I'll send the distress call."

Kira sits next to me on the bench. "I'm okay," I tell her.

"I don't see how," she responds. "I'm not okay. I just figured that we can't freak out 'til we're safe, right?" I smile a little. I don't have anything to say. "What'd you find in his pockets?" Sustenance bar wrappers, a half-eaten something. I drop all that to the ground. A couple flash drives, a polished silver colored ring, too small for his hand. He said his sister gave it to him so he could give it to his girlfriend. Maybe she'd want it back. If I could find her. Maybe Idris could find her. I almost cried when I was assigned to Outpost 16. I had to leave my brothers on Terra 2. They were being sent to advanced classes and couldn't take care of me anymore.

"How's your watch?" Kira asks. I take it out and shake it. It starts ticking again.

"It's okay, Kira," I say. "He didn't die in vain."

"Yeah, I know. It just sucks. We were so close."

"Idris, you have the cure, right?" I ask.

He pats his left hip pocket. "Wouldn't leave home without it. What was he carrying?"

"Not much," I tell him.

"Is that his ring? You might as well put it on. You're the closest thing to a girlfriend he had."

"I'll get it back to his sister."

"Last I heard, she's on Outpost 14." A computer beeps. Kira joins Idris at the control panels.

"What is it?" she asks.

"I think they're scanning for signs of life. We should probably do the same - let them know we're here." Idris presses a couple buttons, a moment, then another beep. "Humans are definitely ahead."

"How far away are they?" I ask.

"Maybe an hour," Idris replies. He steers the pod towards the ships. I lean back and close my eyes. There's too much going on in my head to sleep, but that's all I want to do now. My watch is too big for me, so I put it back in my pocket. Warren's ring fits on my right middle finger. It shouldn't get lost from there.

50.

A gentle shake and "Wake up, Lacy." I don't remember lying down. I have to clear my head before I remember Warren's not here with us. There's a large ship on the monitor.

"Sorry to wake you, kid," Idris says, "but you are our senior officer."

"No problem. Anyone call on the comm yet?"

"We don't even know if they're friendly yet," Kira points out.

"We're about to find out," Idris says, still watching the screen.

"Identify yourself," comes across the pod's speakers.

"You know who we are," Idris responds. "Identify yourself."

"This is Shuttle Terra 4-102. Pod 16-225, you have disconnected without proper authorization. Explain yourself."

"Hi there," I start. "This is Senior Grade 1 Harrison. I need to speak with your commanding officer."

A long pause. "Who is your commanding officer?"

"I am," I respond. "It'd make a whole lot more sense if we could see each other."

Another pause, then "Prepare to be boarded."

"What should we do?" Kira asks quietly.

"We just sit and wait," Idris says just as softly.

The shuttle scrapes our outer hull as it joins with our pod. We're ready with our weapons in case they're hostile.

"I'm only at 30%," Kira points out. "You?"

"I'm at 40," I tell her.

"The point of all this is to take as many of them with us as we can," Idris says. He holds the plasma blaster steady.

The hatch seal is broken, and the door is pulled outward. I really wish my hands would stop sweating. A rifle points at us from the opening, then comes its handler - a nervous security specialist in a green suit, probably a J3.

"Hello. Hi. Can we put these down? What do you say?" He does his best impression of a smile.

"Where is your commanding officer?" Idris snarls.

"Look, I don't want any trouble." The kid sounds a little more sure of himself now. "My orders are to bring your leader to mine. How about we start there?"

"My whole group gets off this boat or none of us do," I tell the newcomer.

He thinks for a moment then lowers his gun. "Okay. We'll try it your way. You go first, and I'll make sure the hatch gets closed."

No stopping 'til we get to the captain running this ship. Warren would have had to duck - this is an old shuttle. Four security officers with guns drawn escort us to the captain. She's probably half a meter taller than me, but she still doesn't quite touch the ceiling.

"Hello," she smiles. "I understand you had a hard time getting here."

"Who's in charge?" I don't feel like repeating myself fifty times tonight.

"That would be me." The smile fades quickly. "And since you are guests here, I have to insist you give up your weapons for the length of your visit." Not that I like it, but we decide to hand over our guns. "Thank you." On her signal, the security officers holster their weapons.

"We need to show something to your scientists," I tell her.

"In due time. I was told we were picking up four people."

"We lost one along the way."

"I'm sorry to hear that. Truly." None of us have an answer for her. "We were also told that there's a possible break in treating OEV?"

"That's what we need to show your scientists," I explain.

"You figured this out?" she almost smiles.

"Are you doubting that a couple senior grades can't develop cures to things?" Idris demands.

"Well, since the best brains on all known human posts have been working on it for over 200 years, forgive me if I'm a little skeptical."

"It's hard to explain," I say. "Look, I promise we're not going to make trouble, okay? We're just really tired," I look to Kira and Idris, "and I'm hungry,"

"Of course," the captain smiles again. "We can talk over a meal." She looks to a lieutenant. "Take our guests to the briefing room. I'll be there in a moment."

The briefing room is made for six people, tops, to sit around a tiny table. We sit, and the door closes after the lieutenant leaves.

"Do we trust her?" Idris asks quietly.

"We don't have a choice," Kira says.

"She knows about us, and she hasn't arrested us or anything," I offer.

"Well, I guess this is it then," Idris sighs. Kira closes her eyes. I sit back, put my feet up on a chair, and wait.

51.

I'm suddenly awake, and nobody else is here. When did I fall asleep? Where did the others go? It takes a minute to remember we're on a shuttle heading somewhere. I don't think we're being detained. I'm still hungry. The door opens - it's the captain.

"We're approaching Terra 4," she says. "We need you to take a seat with your friends."

Everyone else is secured in their entry/exit seats. The captain takes her position with her pilots. I strap myself into the empty space between Kira and Idris.

"You should've woken me up," I tell Idris.

"You didn't miss anything," he says.

"Did you show them the stuff?"

"They thought it'd be best if we looked at it in a real lab."

"They're sending investigators to the station," Kira tells me.

"Good. They can find the fungus for themselves."

"Too bad we never found Warren's hiding place," she says.

"I'm sure they will," I say. "They'll tear the place apart."

The bumpy ride through the atmosphere begins.

"Too bad the Earth man isn't still there," Idris sighs.

"That's okay," Kira smiles. "I mentioned him in one of the messages I sent out."

It's too bouncy for us to talk now, and it feels as if the heat shields are failing.

"Steady," I hear the captain say.

"We're cleared for re-entry," one of the pilot reports. I guess that's good as long as we don't fry to death.

After an eternity, the pilots slow our descent and head to the tiny spaceport to our left. It takes a minute for the air to start blowing cold again. Even Kira's sweating.

"That was fun," Idris mutters, wiping his brow.

The city to the right of the spaceport just keeps getting bigger the closer we get. I wonder what it's like to be with so many people. What if you get lost? There are a lot of green spaces in the city. I know there's a spa here somewhere, but who knew about trees and grass and stuff? If that's what all that is.

The captain swivels her chair around to face us. "Upon landing, you kids will stay with me," she says. "We'll have a security detail, but it's just a formality. Once we report to the chief, we'll head over to the science lab, and then we'll find you someplace to stay."

"Any chance we could stay together?" Kira asks.

"We'll see about that," the captain responds. "You girls certainly shouldn't have a problem, but, Idris, right? We'll see what we can do to keep you close to them."

"Thank you."

"Prepare for docking," a pilot says. The captain turns herself around and locks her chair into place.

"Terra 4-102, it's all you," comes over the speakers. If we slow down any more, we'll crash onto the rocks along the edge of the landing zone. Yet, the pilots put us right over the X. The crew starts unbuckling themselves.

"Is this your first time on a terrapost?" someone in front of us asks.

"Yes," Kira answers.

"You'll need to take it easy for a few days. There's more oxygen here than you're used to."

"Thanks."

"We're down." The pilots turn the engines off and open the hatch. We're the last to unbuckle ourselves. The captain stays behind with us.

"Ready?" she asks.

"Sure," Idris says.

"Welcome to Terra 4."

THE END